Table c

Contents

Christmas Stories

Recipes

MERRY CHRISTMAS

FROM THE AUTHORS

OF EASTERN IDAHO..

Glad Tidings of Great Joy

by River Ames

Nathan decided to take a shortcut across to where his pickup truck was parked. All things considered, he would rather spend that time at his horse ranch than in town on a perfect summer afternoon like today. He stepped onto the grassy, open field, and then halted in mid-step.

A pack of rampaging, exuberant children dashed across the green space. While sneakered small feet kicked at the soccer ball, he noticed that only a few actually connected with the ball. Each successful contact sent the spinning orb flying off onto a new, unpredictable direction.

The band of kids were laughing so hard, it was amazing that any of them actually got their feet within spitting distance of the ball. Clearly no one was keeping score. As far as he could tell, the object of the game was to run full-out, as if they were hounds in pursuit of a highly motivated fox.

Organized mayhem, American style.

This is why you did it, why you served in Afghanistan.

To preserve this way of life.

1

Nathan thought of the stark contrast between these frolicking kids and the solemn-eyed Afghan children he'd encountered during his service.

He hoped that one day they, too, could experience this kind of innocent abandon.

Nathan's gaze drifted to the lone adult managing the jubilant melee. Sunlight spilled across a redheaded woman dressed in a white blouse, knee-length shorts, and white running shoes.

Why were the lyrics of a long-forgotten love song ringing in his head?

"The First Time Ever I Saw Your Face"

Yeah, those were the words!

What did he plan on doing? Just walk up and say, what? You're the woman of my dreams?

Maybe he could join in the game and strike up a casual conversation. He looked down at his feet. Why was he wearing cowboy boots? Oh yeah, he was a cowboy.

A kindly fate took pity on him. One of the kids connected with the soccer ball and sent it flying directly to him.

"Hey mister, give us back our ball."

Nathan discovered that, if he were careful, it was possible to play soccer with leather-tooled boots and a sappy grin on his face.

Gracelyn Hope Snow. He hadn't wasted a minute in learning the wholesome-looking siren's name.

Christmas Eve, one year later.

Friends and even strangers had called him a hero, but he'd seen the pity in their eyes. He would never be the man he'd once been. Gracie needed to be free to find a whole man to love her. And what if they had kids? He could imagine them being embarrassed and ashamed at having a cripple for a father.

He went to the couch and pulled the boot off his right foot, then tugged off his wet sock. Planning ahead, he'd left a towel nearby. He used it to dry off and then massage his cold skin and increase his circulation.

He might be a cripple, but he still could put in a hard day's work.

Nathan leaned back against the sofa. It was his bed nowadays. No way could he torture himself by returning to the bedroom he and Gracie had shared. He looked down at his foot. He couldn't picture any woman wanting to cuddle up to cartoonish monstrosity. A sudden impulse to remove it from him and fling it far away from him was almost overwhelming. He resisted it, of course. After all, a man needed two legs to get around.

He only realized that he'd moved to the front door when his saw his hand moving to turn the doorknob. What was going on? Why did he have this overwhelming compulsion to open the door and look outside?

He looked out and saw, what? A panoramic world of blowing snow industriously building small drifts across the flat yard area.

What else did he expect to see during a Montana blizzard on Christmas Eve?

Looking out into the evening snowstorm, Nathan's logical mind told him that he was a fool. This was crazy. He was freezing for no good reason. He turned to the proffered warmth of his snug abode.

Wait!

The clearly voiced command had Nathan spinning around. "Who's there?"

The living room was as empty as an abandoned tomb. The fine hairs at the nape of his neck stood at attention. The sensation was a familiar one. He'd experienced a few times in Afghanistan. Almost immediately something bad had happened.

By now, he should have learned to listen to "the voice from nowhere" as he'd thought of it.

But, less than a year ago it had remained stubbornly mute, offering no warning when he'd stepped into a convenience store to pick up a gallon of milk. A teenage gunman was holding the clerk and two customers at gunpoint. The terrified gazes of a teenage girl and an older man and woman had looked at Nathan with such aching, pleading eyes that he'd reacted instinctively and rushed forward to knock the punk off his feet and grab the gun.

The pistol had discharged. Nathan had been struck in his thigh, and arterial blood had spurted as if gushing from a broken water pipe. The recovery, as they termed it, had diminished him in

4

phases—first his foot, then his lower leg—until finally he'd been left with a sixteen-inch stump that ended above where his knee had been.

He thought of the life insurance policy he kept making payments on. It would pay off a cool million to his widow even in case of suicide. But he could never do that to Gracie. He knew how her mind and heart worked. She would feel unbearable guilt that she had somehow let him down when the truth was, he'd been the one to let her down.

Lately, he would catch himself daydreaming about ways to make a suicide look like a fatal accident. That way Gracie would be financially set for life and freed from any sense of having failed him. She would mourn his death!

It broke his heart to think of his Gracie grieving. But, surely after a period of time, the emotional pain would lessen, and she would move on with her life.

Afghanistan!

The sweltering heat, the relentless desert. The occasional, unpredictable deadly explosion.

He never knew why he always dreamed of that forsaken place. It had been a desolate wasteland, but he'd made it out alive and in one piece.

Finally, he fell gently and gratefully into slumber. Images flicked rapidly through his weary brain. His conscious mind was awake enough for Nathan to realize he wasn't returning to a barren desert dreamscape. He went willingly. Any place had to be better than here.

"Nathan, get up. Now!"

He bolted upright. He rubbed his eyes. He got to his feet and looked around.

"Go outside."

He almost jumped out of his skin. Someone was messing with him. He jerked his gaze to every darkened corner. Nothing!

Only this time, the voice had been inside his head and not spoken aloud.

He was fully awake now.

He turned the exterior light again and peered outside. He squinted against the blowing snow. Just as his living room had been highlighted in shadows and points of illumination so was the snow-covered landscape. For the first time, he noticed that one of the forming snowdrifts was of a different shape than the others. It seemed to vaguely outline –something. What?

He stepped forward, almost lost his balance, but was able to catch himself. He knelt down beside the mysterious mound. The wildly whipping wind howled as if intent upon utterly extinguishing him.

The still form was Gracie.

The crazy woman had decided to come back to him in the middle of a blizzard.

"Oh, honey! What have you done?"

His hoarse words expelled on a breath of despair. As he frantically brushed the snow from her, his entire body seemed to clench up in dread.

"Let her be all right. Let her live." Then, "I'm sorry, I'm sorry, I'm sorry"

And finally, "Forgive me"

This was all his fault. He'd driven her away with his pride and his bitterness. The way he'd lashed out at her had made it impossible for her to remain and at the same time hold onto her dignity.

He scooped her into his arms and ran in an uneven, clumsy gate. He burst into the house and kicked shut the door.

He got her to the couch and began to pull her sodden clothes from her. Terrified as he'd never been before, not in Afghanistan, not in the Emergency room the night he'd been shot, he touched his fingers to the side of her throat and felt for a pulse.

It was there, faint and barely detectable!

He hadn't known he was crying, until he had to wipe the hot tears from his eyes so that he could see what he was doing

He swept up the blanket from the couch and wrapped her in it before carrying her to the bathroom. She needed immediate warmth to bring up her core body temperature. He held her in one arm while he closed the tub's stopper and turned on the hot water with his other hand. He turned on the cold water also. He knew enough about hypothermia to understand that even though she needed warmth, it would be dangerous to put her in water that was too hot.

She was submerged up to her chin when her eyes opened. The snow covering her head had melted and her wet hair was plastered against her scalp. Her blue eyes appeared huge. Her lips were a darker shade of blue. Somewhere in his mind, he registered that his Gracie was more than a little pregnant.

When her teeth began to chatter, he thought he'd never heard a more joyful sound.

They stared at each other without speaking.

Gracie's whole body was shivering now, and he recognized it as a positive sign. He reached for a bath towel. Lifting her out of the tub, he wrapped her in the terrycloth and carried her into their bedroom.

He knew the moment feeling returned to her feet because she began to sob.

"Sweetheart, I know it hurts," he said, blinking back more tears. "The pain is a good sign."

"I'd hate to see a bad one then," she managed to get out through her chattering teeth.

It took him a moment to figure out what she meant. He shocked himself with a bark of laughter. His Gracie was a fighter.

"The sensation of pins and needles will pass. Having them means you have feeling in your feet."

She shot him a look of furious outrage.

8

"Nathan Spencer Calder, I've decided to give you second chance at showing some common sense."

His heart leapt inside his chest. He briefly closed his eyes.

His thick head got it.

"A second chance is all I want, darling."

Her militant gaze narrowed. "You really mean it and aren't just saying it to humor me?"

A laugh escaped his constricted throat muscles.

"I know a Christmas miracle when I see one, and there's no way I would turn my back on it."

He stared at the definite swell where her flat abdomen had been the last time he'd seen her.

"There's a solid sheet of ice on the sidewalk beneath the new snow."

"I'll do a better job keeping the walk shoveled."

He knew he was smiling as sappily as when he'd begun kicking a soccer ball wearing cowboy boots.

"I promise. You're looking at a man who's very grateful that the love of his life is alive and with him."

She finally smiled.

"That's sweet!"

A change of heart! How is it done?

"I gave you my son, first as a baby and then as the ultimate sacrifice. Through the suffering, death, and resurrection of your Savior, Jesus Christ, all men and women who've lived upon this earth will have their earthly frames transformed to an immortal and perfect state. He'd been born as a helpless baby. Then, he'd grown up and become the Savior of all mankind!

Their Lord had walked the same path all of us travel from infancy, to adulthood, to blessed agedness. And, through the power of His magnificent Atonement all people are given a chance for forgiveness, even a dumb kid who made a mistake that would forever alter the lives of innocent victims.

He bowed his head and said another quick, urgent prayer of gratitude.

Thank you, God!

ABOUT the AUTHOR – RIVER AMES

River Ames spent the first eighteen years of her life in Southern California where she attended twenty-six different elementary schools, two different junior high schools and four different high schools. In one elementary school, she was a student for only three days. Perhaps, because she was so frequently identified as the "new girl," the pattern of River being an observer instead of a participant in the interactions going on around her seemed a logical fit for her personality. After Southern California, River has spent the next part of her life living in the semi-rural town of Idaho Falls, Idaho. She is a graduate of Idaho State University, majoring in Health

Education Sciences and Addiction Counseling. She's worked the past ten years at a Behavioral Health Center where she assisted children, teenagers, and adults committed in a 24/7 secured facility because of mental health challenges they are experiencing. Available Now: "To Each His Own," "Detour to Paradise," "Bachelor in the Boondocks" "Every Good Deed" River's books celebrate the good-natured humor that lays at the core of most of our human predicaments. Readers have said: "In a River Ames book, one minute I'm laughing out loud and the next I have a lump in my throat."

Her books can be found at riverames.com

APPLE DUMPLINGS

submitted by River Ames

This recipe is surely a representation of True Love…

INSTRUCTIONS:

Peel and halve 6 Granny Smith apples.

Core out the center of each half and pat enough brown sugar with a dash of cinnamon to fill each hollow.

Make a pie crust and roll it out.

Place each apple-half into one section of pie crust.

Place the halved apples wrapped in pie-crust into a well-buttered casserole dish. (Place the apples so that the flat section of the apple is face-down, and the smooth, plump side is face up.

Heat to a boil: 1 cup brown sugar

½ cube of butter

1 cup of water

Pour the mixture over the pie-crust-covered dumplings.

Bake at 350 degrees for one hour.

The dumplings are done when the pie crust covering them is a rich, golden brown.

A Child's Eyes

by Shanon Blosch

gaudy reds, royal blues, bright greens

a color fest for little hands

to place as high as we can,

sitting on Dad's shoulder to place the star.

tinsel raining from the sky to land

haphazardly here and there.

Small hands clap in delight and feet dance.

Next comes magic;

the lights glow through boughs

and the tree comes to life.

Eyes brighten and lips round into an O,
one big breath held tight
to be released in a whoosh.
Vocal cords begin to jabber;
wonder and awe flowing freely.

Excitement builds day by day

as pretty paper and bows
fill the space under the tree
enormous packages not easily shaken
fingers itching to take peek.
Time slows to an agonizing crawl;
a visit to Santa should do the trick,
but all we do is wait... and wait... and wait...

Yearly traditions that can't be missed.

store windows with magical scenes,
songs to make us laugh or cry,
handprint trees and macaroni wreaths,
construction paper chains to count the days,
sugar cookies with frosting mountains,
hot cocoa and marshmallows by the fire, and
Rudolph and Frosty on the TV.

Boots and scarves and mittens scattered.

snow drifting up the side of the house and

frost lining the window panes.

Snowmen in scarves to guard the yard;

sleds with red runners abandoned

at the bottom of a white hill,

hard edges softened under mounds

of blinding white sparkles.

Anticipation builds as the big day approaches;

the concept of time has no meaning, and

tempers fray as tears and tantrums come easily.

Is it time? Is it time? Is it time?

Wrapping paper flies and shrieks fill the air,

laughing adults receive thank-yous and hugs and extended family

looks on with love and nostalgia.

The best is yet to come—Santa delivers tonight!

Go to bed! Go to bed! Go to bed!

Cookies and milk left just so

arranged and arranged again;

maybe a quick bite to test for freshness

one last round of hugs and kisses

with a loop around the couch for good measure;

eyes shining in the dark as dreams and wishes
are about to come true.

Waking with a start to a deep silence in the night;

Has he come? Has he come? Has he come?
Creeping down the hall in stockinged feet…
Is it here? Is it here? Is it here?
That one special toy revered above the rest?
Yes! Yes! Oh yes! Joy abounds!
Spinning and spinning and hugging myself in delight;
a movement catches my attention...

What was that? What did I see?

Frozen in wide-eyed wonder
I stare out the window in awe.
There across the street,
through the neighbor's window…
hands cover my mouth as I gasp.
It's him! It's him! It's him! Santa!
Magic lives and breathes.

ABOUT the AUTHOR: SHANON BLOSCH

When she is not writing, you will find Shanon spending time with her amazing family and friends, traveling, reading, or teaching middle school kids English and history. She has been a public-school educator for 28 years.

Shanon Blosch, born and raised in Montana and Wyoming, began writing in high school. With her grandfather as her biggest fan, she created stories through poetry. After a significant break to raise kids, she started writing again in 2013. She loves telling stories through poetry, working to find just the right words to create pictures in readers' minds. Her poetry is often insightful and powerful, sharing deep emotions and hopefully, a new perspective.

Shanon has shared her work through poetry competitions where she frequently places in the top three competitors. Shanon is working on a collection of poems to be published soon.

You can contact her at shanblosch@gmail.com

CRANBERRY BRIE BITES

A favorite of Shanon Blosch

INGREDIENTS

- 1 (8oz) tube crescent dough
- Cooking spray for pan
- Flour, for surface
- 1 (8oz) wheel of brie
- 1/2 cup whole cranberry sauce
- 6 sprigs of rosemary, cut into 1" pieces
- Chopped pecans (optional)

DIRECTIONS

- Preheat oven to 375 degrees and grease a mini (or full) muffin tin with cooking spray.
- On a lightly floured surface, roll out crescent dough (pinch seams if rolls). Cut into 24 pieces for mini muffin pan or 12 for regular muffin pan. Place into muffin pans.
- Cut brie into appropriate sizes based on your muffin pan and place inside crescent dough. Top with a spoonful of cranberry sauce, and one sprig of rosemary. Can add chopped pecans if you wish.
- Bake until crescent dough is golden, about 15 minutes

The Gingerbread Man

by Mary Ann Cherry

It was the gingerbread man that did me in. Somewhere between decorating the ornamental red frosting of the vest with the colorful gumdrop buttons and plunking on the crinkly raisin eyes, my own peepers began to leak. When the first tear fell, I told myself it would soon pass by like a short spring rain.

I was—although I seldom am—wrong.

Perhaps it was because it was mid-December, not spring, that the first tear became a trickle and the trickle became an outright salty downpour. Why, I fair drowned out Elvis on the radio, and him singing my favorite Blue Christmas. I'm just saying, that if me and Elvis had been having a contest on blue, I had him whipped like the frosting on those gingerbread cookies. You could pick any color of blue out of the crayon box and I knew down to my woolly socks how that color felt.

And I'm not—because I seldom am—lying.

It had been six months since my husband died and eight months since my mother had passed on to that great place in the sky. It seemed like Christmas should have the courtesy to somehow just go away. Disappear. Instead, here I was, frosting gingerbread cookies just like mom and I had done when I was a child. Like nothing had happened and mom and Ted would just walk in the door at any minute and POOF, life would be normal. I looked that cookie in the eye and wondered how I was supposed to pull off a pleasant, family Christmas. I swear that little brown man gave me back the fish eye. Damn his gingery, cinnamon-smelling hide.

What was Kami thinking bringing her family home for Christmas? Did my girl not have the sense God gave a carrot? My gosh, at least a carrot starts out orange, stays orange and remains so when you cook it. Orange.

Kami started out with good common sense, went all flighty—flighty—when she met that man, married him and moved to France like nobody but she and that man mattered bo-diddly. Like having her move to France wasn't like ripping my beating heart right out of my chest. (Which would be quite a job because I'm pretty blessed in that department, just saying.) And now, here she was trotting back at Christmas with a child I never even laid eyes on. After nearly six long years. Not the common sense of a carrot.

Of course, here we were. We three—me, myself and I—frosting gingerbread men for that little boy—a total stranger I never even got to hold when he was born. Or when he had his first birthday. Or his second. Or his…well, you get the picture. So maybe I didn't have the common sense of a root vegetable either. Probably where Kami gets it from.

The upshot of it was, I missed my mom. Here I stood in my bright kitchen with the red-checkered wallpaper and country curtains with the hens and roosters on the fabric. (I never quite figured out why there were so many roosters when everyone knows a barnyard only needs one. Some textile designer who didn't know his chickens was getting paid good money for that lack in her education.) And I missed my mom so much it fairly hurt to breathe. Like I couldn't get enough air. I missed her cheerful smile and the sparkle of her eyes. The love she poured out like honey over Sunday flapjacks.

I missed being someone's little girl. And it was Christmas.

I know, I know. You think I should be missing Ted, that louse, that out and out bounder of a big no-good specimen of manhood. Well, you'd be wrong. He'd been as much of a mistake as that man my Kami had strolled down the aisle with. Calling my husband a philandering skunk would be a kindness.

And I'm not—because I seldom am—exaggerating.

22

Frankly, since he's dead and six feet under I don't see a reason to be polite. Politeness and forgiveness and turning the other cheek and all that might be Christian, but it's overrated.

I was at the point of mopping my eyes and giving myself a swift mental kick in the tuckus when the doorbell rang and I knew—in pilot lingo—that we had lift off. It would be Kami and that man and my five-year-old grandson I had never seen. Never seen! Like grandmothers weren't important enough to be invited to board a plane and take a trip to France to meet the new member of the family.

I knew that wily gingerbread boy was fairly aching to push me toward the door. If I'd frosted him some lips on his devious little head he'd be yelling, "Answer the blasted door before I go deaf, you crazy woman!"

So, I did.

It was the UPS man. You know, he's sort of a jerk, but he's a good-looking, kindly jerk. He's got twinkly blue eyes, dark brown hair not even going grey yet. And well, he's got some muscles on him from hauling around all those packages all day, every day. A whole UPS truckload of muscles.

Not that I was looking--because I never do.

Along with my package he handed me a Christmas card—my first one of the season. I ran back into the kitchen and snatched a gingerbread boy from the counter and presented it to him with a flourish that—well, flourished.

"Brandon," I said, not looking at his muscles, "This is for you. Merry Christmas. But if you don't mind, I wish you'd bite the head off this sucker right now, because I'm in a foul mood and it'll make me feel a whole lot better. If this cookie had a mouth, it would be one of those backtalkers."

So, he did.

He might have planted a quick kiss on my cheek after he chomped into that cookie, too, but I probably made that up on the spur of the moment just to keep you interested in my story. A little flirtation, you know, gets the reader excited about reading on to the next page.

Not that I make things up—because I never do.

After he left, I looked at the package. It was from my aunt Helen. I tore it open and inside there was a small box wrapped in red and green tissue paper with blue snowmen and on top of the whole gaudy mess was a scrawled note that said:

Christmas might be a might tough this year, dear girl. Especially since Kami's husband lost his job and they'll be counting on you to make Christmas a good one for little Jeremy. I thought this photo might brighten your day and help you remember the wonderful time we had when you were small. Love always, Helen

Carefully wrapped in the tissue paper was a framed photo of my aunt, my mother and myself at Christmas. I held a ginger cookie in one hand and had a smear of pink frosting across one cheek. I was about five, the same age my grandson was now. My heart swelled with memories of those wonderful days when life was simpler. When I was still someone's little girl. And with that memory came the thought that it was now my turn.

My turn.

That man had lost his job?

Why hadn't they told me?

My daughter needed me. That sweet grandson of mine needed me. And so did that man who swept my carrot-brained daughter off her feet six years before. My family needed me. In my heart, I knew I needed them more.

Running to the bedroom, I pulled on a never-worn hideous Christmas sweater Kami had sent me two years before. Then I bustled around the kitchen putting cider and mulling spices in a pot to simmer and fill the house with the smell of the holiday. I plugged in the tree lights and put a platter of sugar cookies, gingerbread men and gumdrops on the coffee table.

Elvis was singing *White Christmas* when the doorbell rang. And I had on that ugly sweater and an elf hat that looked plum puddin' ridiculous. I thought I heard one of the gingerbread men snicker, then whisper, sweet as molasses, "So go answer it already, Lady!"

So, I did.

That man, that sweet, lovely, generous man, stood on the porch with my daughter and grandson. My family was home for Christmas.

ABOUT the AUTHOR: MARY ANN CHERRY

Award winning mystery author, Mary Ann Cherry, is a professional artist, much like the heroine, Jessie O'Bourne, in her writing—that is, the writing she normally does when not asked to produce a short story. She was raised in rural Montana in an area like the fictitious town of Sage Bluff in her novels, and now lives in rural Idaho with her husband and several pudgy cats. Cherry is working on book three of her series.

When Cherry isn't writing, she travels to art shows, where she exhibits her paintings professionally and takes part in 'quick draws', producing a painting in about an hour's time from start to finish. Her work is in the permanent collection of several art museums, and she is a Master Signature/Emeritus member of the Women Artists of the West and 2019-2020 president.

Usually, you can find her painting in her home studio or slaving away at her writing desk on an upper-floor landing—one that affords a lovely view of a grassy yard and a lush golden willow tree during the summer and frost covered branches and snow during those cold Idaho winters. Wherever she is working, the coffee pot is always on and the brew is of the good strong Norwegian variety that holds up the spoon.

GINGERBREAD MEN

INGREDIENTS

- 1 cup shortening
- 1 cup granulated sugar
- 1 egg
- 1 cup molasses

- 5 cups sifted all-purpose flour
- 1 ½ teaspoons soda
- ½ teaspoon salt
- 2 to 3 teaspoons ground ginger
- 1 or 2 teaspoons ground cinnamon
- 1 teaspoons ground cloves

INSTRUCTIONS

- Cream shortening and sugar together
- Beat in egg, molasses and vinegar
- Sift together dry ingredients and blend in
- Chill 3 hours

Roll the dough ¼ inch thick on a lightly floured surface. Cut into shapes. Place one inch apart on a greased cookie sheet. Bake at 375 degrees for 5 to six minutes. Cool slightly before removing to rack. Makes about four dozen but it depends on the size of your cookie cutter. These are good all year long in any shape!

FROSTING: I prefer a simple buttercream frosting

- 6 tbsp butter
- One 1-pound pkg of confectioner's sugar (about 4 ¾ cups sifted)
- Light cream or half 'n half (approximately ¼ cup
- 1 ½ teaspoons of vanilla

Make several colors of frosting so that you can decorate them with little vests or faces, etc. and be sure to add some raisin eyes and/or buttons!

BEST DINNER ROLLS ...Yields approx. 20 dinner rolls

INGREDIENTS

- 1/2 cup flour
- 2 teaspoons active dry yeast
- 1/2 cup lukewarm water
- 2 eggs
- 1/2 cup plain Greek yogurt
- 2 tablespoons sugar

- 1/4 cup water
- 3 1/4 cups flour
- 4 tbsp melted and slightly cooled butter
- 2 tbsp salted butter (for brushing the rolls, optional)

INSTRUCTIONS

1. In your stand-up mixing bowl, mix 1/2 cup flour, 1/2 cup lukewarm water and the dry yeast. Mix to combine and

leave at room temperature until bubbly and has a sponge-like texture.

2. In a separate bowl whisk the eggs with the yogurt, salt, sugar and the remaining 1/4 cup water.

3. Fit mixer with dough hook and turn on to the lowest speed.

4. With the mixer running, add the wet ingredients to the yeast mixture. It's going to be a very sticky batter.

5. Gently, on the lowest speed, add the 3 1/4 cups of flour, little by little.

6. When all the flour is added pour the 4 tbsp of melted butter and slowly increase the mixer' speed from low to high.

7. Keep mixing for 2-3 minutes and turn the mixer off. With a wooden spoon or a spatula, clean the sides of the bowl, scraping down the sticky dough.

8. Turn the mixer back on and mix on medium-to-high for another 2-3 minutes or until the dough will start to clean itself from the sides of the bowl. It's still going to be little sticky, <u>don't be tempted to add flour</u>.

9. With the help of a spatula/wooden spoon put the dough into a clean buttered bowl, cover with plastic wrap and leave at room temperature for about 1 1/2 hours or until doubled in volume.

10. Punch down the dough and, with floured hands, take the dough out of the bowl and place it on a floured surface.

11. Now divide the dough into 20 pieces, shaping each one into a ball. Place them on baking sheet (at this point you can wrap tightly in plastic and freeze for future use) cover again with plastic wrap or a tea towel and leave at room temperature for another 30-40 minutes.

12. Meanwhile, heat the oven to 375F.

13. Bake the rolls for about 20 minutes or until golden.

14. As soon as you take them out of the oven brush them with the salted butter.

15. Enjoy!

The Christmas Truce

An excerpt from
BRANDENBURG: A STORY of BERLIN

by James Cloud

S*tille Nacht, heilige Nacht, alles schläft, einsam Wacht...*"

Eckhardt heard men's voices singing from somewhere down the trench line. He had been dozing as he rested in his bunker in a German trench on the Western Front near Verdun, Belgium. Upon completion of their training in early September, he and Herbert had taken part in the First Battle of the Marne, where Germany's drive through Belgium had been halted. The armies had then been bogged down, which resulted in the beginning of trench warfare. This led to the development of a meandering line of trenches extending for several hundred miles from the northern coast of Belgium near the Dutch border to the Swiss border near Basel.

Within hours of the beginning of the battle, rain began to fall and continued throughout the first five months of the war. The

32

battlefield soon turned into a quagmire and the soldiers found themselves standing in cold water sometimes over their boot tops. However, shortly before Christmas Eve, the rain stopped, and the temperature dropped below freezing. In the higher places the water had drained out of the trenches and the ground became solid. After being able to rotate to the rear and dry out their clothing and receive hot food and coffee, the men were grateful for the cessation of the rain in spite of the colder temperature.

As he came out of the bunker, Eckhardt realized that in addition to the beloved hymn being sung in German, he was hearing a response of "Silent Night, Holy Night" being sung in English by the British troops in their trench less than 100 yards away. As he walked along the trench, he saw some of his comrades placing small Christmas trees with lit candles on the parapet. Some were even standing up in full view of their adversaries, some of whom were doing the same. "What's going on here?" he enquired of a soldier standing nearby.

"Someone further down the line began shouting 'Merry Christmas' in English to the Tommies over there," the man responded. "Then the singing started, and now I hear that both sides are discussing a cease fire."

At this, Eckhardt saw several soldiers raising signs with the message, 'You no shoot–we no shoot.' "Incredible!" Eckhardt exclaimed. "I wish Herbert were here to see this." Herbert having contracted a serious case of dysentery two weeks previously, had been sent to a field hospital several miles from the front.

The other soldier did not respond as he climbed the small ladder leading to the top of the trench, and with many others began to walk across No Man's Land toward the British lines. British Tommies were doing the same, and the two groups met and began to shake hands and talk. Some of the Germans had worked in England before the war and could converse surprisingly well in English. Occasionally one could hear a conversation which revealed that a German was familiar with the hometown of his British conversation partner.

After some hesitation, Eckhardt decided to join the group between the two trench lines. He climbed up the ladder and walked across the rough terrain of No Man's Land, which was strewn with barbed wire. Shortly thereafter, he encountered a young Englishman who appeared to be about the same age as himself. The young man smiled hesitantly and extended his hand to Eckhardt. They shook hands warmly and began to converse in a mixture of broken English and German. Soon it became clear that an interpreter would be needed. Standing near a group where much English was being spoken, Eckhardt asked an older German, who appeared to be fluent in the language, if he could help out.

"Certainly, son. Glad to." The man introduced himself as a member of one of the Saxon regiments from further down the line.

"Where did you learn to speak such good English?", Eckhardt enquired of the man.

"I was a barber in Liverpool for almost ten years. I really enjoyed England, and the Brits are really alright fellows. It's a real tragedy that we're fighting each other now. I would have stayed there, except for this damned war. But when it started, I couldn't turn my back on the fatherland, and so I came back to serve, and here I am," the man concluded with a look of sadness.

Eckhardt found this very perplexing. He wondered what he would have done in the same situation.

"You and your new Limey friend need shearing. Let me give you a haircut–on the house. I carry my clippers and scissors with me everywhere. A Christmas present to you both." He then repeated the same offer to the Englishman in his language. After being seated on a nearby crate, both young men were soon handsomely groomed, for which they both responded with gratitude.

With the help of their older friend, they were introduced to each other and learned that they were both from small country towns: William from Calne in Wiltshire, and Eckhardt from Blaubeuren in Wuerttemberg. They showed one another photographs of their families, and also pictures of their respective sweethearts. Eckhardt proudly showed him Ursula's photo which she had sent in a letter soon after he and Herbert had left Berlin.

The young Englishman displayed the picture of a pretty delicate-featured girl named Elizabeth.

Soon the suggestion began to make the rounds that they should use this special opportunity to collect their dead comrades, some of whom had been lying on the ground and entangled in barbed wire for days, weeks, and even in many cases months. Due to natural decomposition of the corpses, and additionally to them having been eaten by the rats which infested the trenches and battlefields, this was a gruesome task, but one which both sides agreed should be undertaken. They collected the remains, and where possible grouped them in their respective nationalities, but when identification could no longer be determined, they were placed in common graves, thereby consigning them to resting places with Germans and Englishmen lying together. Prayers were offered in both languages, and the feeling of common humanity was felt by all present.

After the burials were completed, the men began to exchange souvenirs, uniform buttons and helmets being especially popular items. Then as the night continued, holiday foods began to make their appearance, the commodities having been provided by the armies of both sides. Roast goose, Westphalian ham, Corned Beef, plum puddings, cakes and breads of various kinds were brought forth and accompanied by beer and liquors of many varieties. After having eaten their fill, and sampling each other's traditional holiday specialties, they became thoughtful and a wistfulness settled over the gathering as they considered the tragedy of their situation, and the necessity of returning to battle and to the slaughtering of one another. The night was cold and clear, and they gazed at the stars, which they knew were shining on their homes and loved ones. Then they began to return to their trenches and prepare to resume the business of taking one another's lives.

ABOUT the AUTHOR: JAMES CLOUD

James Cloud was born and brought up in New Mexico shortly before the outbreak of World War II.

Cloud's first grade teacher in 1943 was Jewish. Minerva Kohn was a loved and respected woman in Las Vegas, New Mexico. His memories of her led to an interest in Jewish culture and traditions. At the same time, his circle of friends and acquaintances included many people from the German-American community. The effects of World War II had a profound influence on him, leading to a lifelong fascination with these two cultures. He also developed friendships with many Jewish people during his years in Boston, where he worked at the Gillette Company.

The author attended the Institute of Arts in West Berlin during the Cold War years. While working as an interpreter, he developed an intimate knowledge of both East and West Berlin. Cloud later completed a Master's Degree in German Linguistics and Literature at California State University in Fullerton.

More than forty years of teaching German and English as a Second Language brought him in contact with people of many nationalities and cultures. Cloud has attempted to bring together in this novel his impressions gained from interactions with these groups—most especially with German and Jewish people—and how they in turn have related to each other.

James Cloud's award-winning novel BRANDENBURG: A STORY OF BERLIN is available on Amazon and on his website at Jamescloudbooks.com. He is currently working on book two of the series.

Frohe Weinachten!

Camouflage Christmas

by Becky Cook

When my children were younger, I started doing the twelve days of Christmas with them. We would choose several families and then put together a plan of implementation involving the sneaky delivery of a gift each of the 12 nights leading up to Christmas Eve to each of the chosen families. The kids were excited to figure out a way to drop the packages off without getting caught, and that is where the adventure started each year.

The very first year we learned just how sneaky we had to be in order to get away without getting caught. We had a family with a large front yard without trees and the first couple of times we dropped things off they weren't home. No problem. But the day came when they were home and we had to change our plans to get that package delivered.

My son dressed up in all white camouflage in order to remain hidden against the snow in the yard. He had me drop him off and slowly circle the subdivision before returning to pick him up. He carefully snuck up the steps, set the package down and knocked, then ran like crazy. He made it to the front of the property where there was a slight dip and he dove into the snow and got as still as possible. The door opened. One of the kids looked outside, picked up the package, and then slowly closed the door.

Mission accomplished. Adrenalin rush achieved.

But it got a LOT harder. Once kids know that there is a possibility that they can catch Santa in the act they start lying in wait. I think that son aged ten years just making it through the final days until Christmas Eve. After a while he just wanted to set the package down and sneak off without ringing the doorbell but the challenge often had him ringing it at the last moment.

He became an adrenaline junkie, using all possible methods to avoid detection and proudly proclaiming that he had never been caught. But all good things come to an end sometime…

The next year there was another family with several kids and several near misses. After that my oldest son took it upon himself to do extensive reconnaissance before allowing any of his sisters to do the drop offs.

On one such occasion, the smallest of the sisters really wanted to help deliver the package. She assured everyone that she could handle the suspense and would drop the package off carefully. Her older brother talked her through the procedure and her sisters helped get her all dressed up in warm winter clothing, including sneakers to run through the snow.

Ah, but the best laid plans can sometimes go awry. Such was the case here.

She only made it two steps outside the car when her sneaker fell off in a snowdrift. It wouldn't have been too much of a problem, but the sneaker was white and the snow was white. The older sister got out of the car and frantically searched around in the snow for the errant sneaker while the next of the younger sisters held the package. Alas, this sister hadn't received the extensive drill down of information. She ran ahead and she was still holding the package when she rang the doorbell. Her sisters were frozen in disbelief, one with a shoe still off in the snowdrift somewhere.

The kids in the house had been waiting anxiously to see if they could catch the mysterious benefactor who left the gifts and they were on the kids like a duck on a June bug.

"We caught you! We knew it had to be someone like you!"

My children protested to no avail—the family kids were sure they had the right people. At least, until later that night when I sneakily delivered ANOTHER gift, with the appropriate note attached saying the package had been delayed.

See, the first gift could be explained away as a family visit to friends since the note that should have been attached was still in someone's pocket. At the very least, it threw some confusion on the issue. My other children would hear the kids from that family talking at school and on the bus and they were thoroughly confused—thinking they knew who was doing the drop, but then getting a second package with a note excusing the lateness of the gift...

Such fun...

Then came the toughest of all assignments. Initially, this family looked to be one of the easiest to deliver to. They had an extensive forest of pine trees in the front yard that gave ample protection to the kid who was delivering the package.

My son chose to deliver the package one night with me. We went out just after sundown, about the fourth day of Christmas. He was dressed in full camouflage, both to keep warm and to lessen the chance of discovery. I dropped him off a short distance from the house and then waited in the warm car for what seemed like a long time. I had my window slightly cracked open to listen to see if I could hear his stealth and honestly didn't hear anything.

Until the scream, that is.

I immediately perked up and within seconds my son came racing out of the trees,

"Floor it, Mom!" he panted.

I carefully eased out of the shelter of the pine trees and turned the car away from the house to avoid detection.

"What happened back there? I heard a scream—was that you?"

"No!" he looked so upset. "I will NEVER do the 12 days of Christmas ever again!"

"Why, what happened?" I questioned, figuring something dire must have happened that he just wasn't telling me.

"Oh mom, it was awful!" he said. "You know how she has all of the cats?"

42

I nodded.

"I had just barely snuck up to the doorstep with the package and seriously had just stretched out my hand to ring the doorbell when she opened the door with a plate of cat food. She saw me and screamed, dropped the food, the cats jumped on it and I fell over them when I came off the steps – it was horrible! I'm never doing the 12 days of Christmas ever again!"

Poor lady! Poor son!

He held to his promise and wouldn't deliver the packages anymore that year and he wouldn't let his sisters either, saying they would be scarred for life like he was.

The 12 days of Christmas had just been abandoned due to cats.

It was several months later when I ventured into a conversation with this particular lady, easing into it with a random comment about Christmas surprises.

"You know, I had the strangest thing happen to me last year," she said. "I opened the door to feed the cats and there was a man there with his face covered, in full camouflage. He threw something at me and jumped off the porch over the cats. I don't know what he was doing but he scared me out of two year's growth! I was afraid to feed the cats in the dark after that!"

I never did tell her the truth about the 12 days of Christmas and the undelivered package. Silence makes the best camouflage...

ABOUT the AUTHOR: BECKY COOK

This story is a complete departure from the standard fare that Becky Cook is known for. To readers all around the United States she is known for her agricultural knowledge, as she has been published in 25 publications—local, regional, and national. She is also well known in the Bigfoot world where she has three books out— BIGFOOT LIVES in IDAHO, BIGFOOT STILL LIVES in IDAHO, and BIGFOOT LIVES FOREVER in IDAHO.

Her books can be found on Amazon, beckycookonline.com, and Bigfootlives.com.

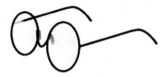

What My Eyes Didn't See

by Becky Cook

Christmas music floated around me from the surrounding streets where I was standing in front of my apartment with a jumble of keys in my hand. I was trying to figure out which one fit the key hole when the girl came up behind me like a mugger. She startled me as if I had been shot.

It isn't as though I can't see, but I just had surgery on my eyes and the doctor sent me home in a cab with instructions not to take the bandages off without dire consequences. As a businessman, it is often difficult to schedule needed appointments, so I had waited until the Christmas break to get some eye surgery done. That might have been fine from a business perspective, but I didn't think it through very well as it left me with no one to help me after surgery after the taxi dropped me off. So, I was stuck there like a little kid, ready to bawl my eyes out from frustration when this woman comes up behind me.

"You want help?" she asks.

I normally don't talk to strangers, but this time I'm up a creek without a Seeing Eye dog… Well, you know what I mean.

"Yeah, sure," I said. "It should be a bigger key for the dead bolt with a smaller key beside it for the main doorknob."

Calmly and efficiently she opened the door as though she'd been living there a while, and just as calmly, she took the newly delivered bag of groceries out of my arms and went on into the apartment.

"I can handle everything from here," I stated.

"Yeah, and probably almost as good as the doorknob," she said. "Don't try and be a he-man or whatever, I'll just help you put these things away."

I fumbled my way into the living area where I was sure I could find the easy chair by myself and then reached over to turn on the light out of habit.

"Thanks for the light," she said, coming up behind me.

I wasn't sure what I was getting myself in to with a strange woman in the house and me not being able to see if she took the silverware or whatever.

"In case you are wondering, I'm not a thief," she said.

I must have flinched or something. Can she read minds too?

"For one thing you don't have anything worth stealing, and for another I'm just trying to be a good citizen," she said. "Do you want a drink of lemonade or something stronger?"

"Uh, lemonade sounds good right now," I said.

"Great, put your hand up."

I nervously put up my hand and felt relieved when she put one of my own large tumblers into it.

"It's not going to bite you," she said. "Are you always this nervous around women?"

Maybe she can read minds.

"Look, I didn't invite you in here, you can at least stop insulting me in my own house," I protested.

"Well, since I am not going to be here very long you can stop being all nervous for a while. I am not going to bite you or anything. Although," she paused... "You do look good in that shade of blue. I might be tempted to just nibble."

Then she laughed at my discomfort. I heard her walk back into the kitchen and there were various noises associated with dinner preparations. I figured I might as well relax as she wasn't going to do me any harm.

I must have dozed off because the next thing I knew she was sitting on my lap. She reached up and held my head still and kissed me then, full on the lips.

Besides the shock of the physical contact where I wasn't expecting any, there was a supercharged moment when I swear a lightning bolt had found its way into my house and hit my heart.

"I'm sorry," she whispered. "I intended to just nibble but you looked so good there I just had to get a bite…er, kiss."

She wiggled around and made motions to get off my lap, but I'm not as stupid as I sometimes look. I just held her all the tighter.

"Isn't there an ad somewhere that says, 'No one can eat just one'," I whispered near what I figured was her ear.

"Those are potato chips or something," she whispered back. "Why are we whispering?"

"Someone might hear us and interrupt," I whispered back, "And you wouldn't want that now, would you?"

"Not just now," she said as she curled back into my arms.

I spent the next few minutes just taking in her essence, from the clean smelling hair to the remnants of perfume that drifted near her like springtime lilacs. Then I just had to kiss her a few times myself.

"Wow," she said. "You aren't slow once you get started, are you?"

"Who says I am slow?" I asked as I nibbled her ear.

"Well, let's consider the evidence."

She sat up a little more primly, still in my lap.

"You are forty-three next month and haven't been married."

I really startled then. She must be a mind reader.

48

"Rumor has it that you don't date, but the same rumor has it that you aren't shy, just slow."

I stood up so abruptly that she fell with a thump to the floor.

"Who are you?" I demanded.

"Just a good Samaritan who opened your door and fixed you dinner," she said. "I'll be going now."

She slid past me with a whisper of cloth, and then she was gone, taking her essence of clean hair and lingering aroma of lilacs. I was left with a bandage over my eyes, needing another one for my heart.

***

Weeks passed, my eyes healed, and I started looking for my mystery Samaritan everywhere. I wasn't sure where I should look for this woman who made such an impact on me, all I had to go on was her height and the perfume of lilacs that she was wearing. That wasn't much to go on…

Long after my eyesight had healed, I continued the search among my colleagues for the woman who had left the imprint on my heart. For the first time in my life, I started to actively date, thinking that perhaps one of those women would graciously drop the fact that she had once opened my door and touched my heart.

"You've really had your eyes opened," my sister taunted me when I asked her if she knew the woman. "Where haven't you looked?"

I slowly listed my dates for her with her nods of approval and an occasional comment of astonishment. When I had finished the list, she looked at me appraisingly.

"I wouldn't have believed it possible that my brother could fall so fast and hard and still miss the real picture," then she giggled.

"What?" I demanded. "You must know something that you haven't told me!"

She looked deep into my eyes and then said, "Honey, did you have them recheck your eyes at a follow up appointment or did you skip that during your mad rush to find this woman?"

All of a sudden, I realized that perhaps she was onto something. I had skipped my follow up appointment with the eye doctor as I was feeling great by then and life got busy. I excused myself right then and made the phone call.

"Doctor's office," she said.

"I'd like to set a date to see you again," I stated.

"I'm sorry sir, but all of our immediate openings are taken, unless..." she paused.

"Unless what?" I asked.

"Unless you want to set up a private time after hours," this came out at nearly a whisper, the same whisper that she used while sitting on my lap.

"How about tonight," I asked. "I'm sure you know how to find the place."

"What place?"

"The place you left my heart when my eyes couldn't see."

ABOUT the AUTHOR: BECKY COOK

This story is a complete departure from the standard fare that Becky Cook is known for. To readers all around the United States she is known for her agricultural knowledge, as she has been published in 25 publications—local, regional, and national. She is also well known in the Bigfoot world where she has three books out— BIGFOOT LIVES in IDAHO, BIGFOOT STILL LIVES in IDAHO, and BIGFOOT LIVES FOREVER in IDAHO.

Her books can be found on Amazon, beckycookonline.com, and Bigfootlives.com.

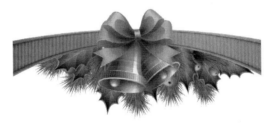

CRESCENT ROLLS

submitted by Becky Cook

INGREDIENTS

- 2 cups hot water
- 2 cubes butter
- 1 cup sugar
- 1 ½ tsp salt
- 2 Tablespoons yeast in ½ cup water, allow to proof
- 6 eggs
- 8-9 cups flour

INSTRUCTIONS

Cut up butter cubes in hot water, allow to melt. Add sugar and salt and mix together. Add eggs all at once along with ½ of the flour, mix. Then add yeast and water mixture and the rest of the flour, knead well about 5-10 minutes (a very important step!)
Set in warm kitchen and allow to rise double.

Divide into five balls and roll out each ball individually into a circle. Cut like a pizza – you should get 16 slices. Brush melted butter on top and then roll from the fat end to the skinny end. Let rise again for 20 minutes and then bake at
350 for 10-12 minutes each pan. Makes 80 crescent rolls. This recipe can be cut in half but I should warn you that we never seem to have leftovers!

Six at Ten

You were holding

The angel doll

Who bends her head

To pray silent night

In the enchanted toyland

Where we are each

Six at ten am

On Christmas morn.

By noon four birds sit

In a bare bough

Outside my empty table

Where I will not burn candles

Nor watch you blow them out.

I shake the red tablecloth,

Line up the washed silver

And fold chocolate bows.

This you have yet to learn:
Some days Christmas
Is a gift we give to others.
You may not ever
Have to know;
You surely do not need to know
When you are six at ten
On a December morn.

—Karen Finnigan

Swedish Cookies

a favorite of Karen Finnigan

- 1/2 cup butter
- 1/4 cup brown sugar
- 1 egg yolk
- 1 cup flour
- Glazed cherries
- Chopped walnuts

Mix butter, sugar, egg yolk & flour. Roll dough into small balls. Dip each into slightly beaten egg white. Then dip into chopped walnuts. Bake 5 minutes at 325 degrees.

Remove from oven and press the center of each with a thimble. Add half a glazed cherry & bake 10 minutes longer. Cool and serve on a cookie plate.

The Changeling

by Karen Finnigan

When I was very young, my dearest wish was for a sibling. But by the time I entered first grade, it seemed it was not to be. Then, one day as the leaves were turning colors, my parents informed me that a new baby was coming soon. I squealed with joy. At once Mother put a finger over my lips and made me promise to tell no one.

I knew why. It was so the trolls could not find out and plot to switch out our new baby. Mother in particular, after many false alarms, was superstitious about this. So much so she would not even set out baby Jesus in his manger before Christmas Eve. Trolls were a part of our heritage. As much as lefse, smoked herring, and skis.

My parents were immigrants who'd arrived here in America shortly before I was born. I knew little of Norway, the old country they'd left, except for the tissue-thin letters with foreign stamps and

58

occasional brown paper packages, stamped with *God Jul* under the stamps. My father worked at the lumber mill, my mother cooked and sewed dresses for me. It was this new life that I orbited.

"I won't tell," I promised. Besides, the girls at school talked at recess about Santa Claus and their desire for sleek-figured high-heeled dolls with eye makeup. It would not be hard to keep our secret and keep the trolls at bay. Based on the reaction to my sack lunch of sardine sandwiches, I suspected that stories about trolls would get me laughed at. Again.

"So *Jul* is coming. Christmas is coming," Mother reminded me. What did I want? I was not to be distracted. All I wanted was a baby, a real live doll of my own.

"Maybe chocolate and nuts and candy cane in my stocking would be nice too," I added.

Mother smiled, and together we decorated a tree with popcorn chains and silver bells and little red yarn gnomes from Norway. Then she pulled out a wicker bassinet from the attic space above our apartment and placed it near the tree, right next to brown paper parcels that were coming early from Norway, from relatives I had never seen or met. Some were squishy, some rattled, but none were as exciting this year as the coming baby.

My baby brother, Jon, was born the week before Christmas and came home on Christmas Eve. That evening as we sat enjoying the lights of the tree, mother laid him, sleeping, in the bassinet. Father offered to move the bassinet to the bedroom, but mother hushed him. "It looks so perfect," she said in a contented voice. "A perfect baby on Christmas Eve."

"Don't let the trolls get jealous," father said.

"Shush," said mother. "Enough of that," and she knelt down to shake one of the brown paper packages.

We used to open them on Christmas Eve, in the Scandinavian custom. But tonight, mother shook her head and put the present back under the tree. This year, because of the new baby, we would wait and open in the morning, the way most of my friends did. While father watched the sleeping baby, she put me in my snowflake nightgown, and we carefully hung my stocking on my doorknob. It was not Santa I thought of as I fell asleep. It was the trolls. Was father right? Would they be jealous? The baby, not yet baptized, was still vulnerable to trolls.

When I awoke it was very early, the apartment chilly, and outside my window a wintry moon shone up in the sky. I looked at the door, still open, and my stocking, hanging on the knob. It was lumpy with nuts and candy. Santa had come and filled it. But nuts and candy that year did not compete with the new baby. I slipped out of bed and tiptoed to the bassinet, which had still not been moved to my parents' room. The room was lit, but the house was quiet. One of the brown paper packages had been torn open. I stepped on coarse paper, and string caught in my toes. I looked in the bassinet and gave a start.

It was not empty, but it was not our new baby who lay there. It was someone strange. My heart clenched.

It was not glamorous. It was not a perfect baby with down hair and silken features. It was a plastic and fabric doll. A stuffed chunky girl doll with long white blond braids. The face was embroidered with puffy blue eyes, a brown button nose, and a crooked mouth. It was dressed in a skirt and blouse of red and black felt with a white apron. There was a tear at her wrist, and a speck of stuffing was coming lose. It did not in any way resemble the glamorous dolls my friends had requested. Nor was it my baby brother.

A changeling. It had to be a changeling.

I knew at once Mother's fears had come true. The trolls had been here during the night. They had hitched a ride on Santa's sleigh; that would have been easy. And they had stolen our perfect baby boy. Tiny little Jon. I burst into tears and called out for my mother.

It was father who came while pulling on a shirt. "Go back to bed," he said gently. "It is too early. It is not time yet. Mother is tired and needs to rest more."

He didn't act as if anything were wrong, so I sobbed louder. "The trolls were here," I said, pointing at the bassinet. "They took our baby. See, there's a changeling. Make it go away. I don't like it."

"Rowena," my mother called as a lamp in her bedroom switched on. I ran to her and could see then she was sitting in a rocking chair in the corner and was holding my baby brother. She handed the bundle of blue to father and took me in her arms.

"There are no trolls," she said in a soothing voice. Her hand brushed my hair back. "There are no trolls."

No trolls?

"But you said…"

"It was all in fun," she said. "We tell troll stories, your father and I, because we are homesick sometimes. We miss the julenissen and troll stories of the old country. But there are none, not really."

I was not entirely convinced. "Then how did the changeling get here?"

"What changeling?" Mother asked.

"I told you we should have moved it," Father said.

Mother put a finger to her lips to quiet Father.

"There is a strange baby in the bassinet," I stammered. "I thought the trolls stole our baby and left the funny doll instead."

"Funny? Why is it funny?"

She walked with me to the tree and we looked at the changeling. No one in school would have a doll like this. I would be laughed at again.

"It is a doll in the Norwegian costume," Mother explained. "It is not funny. It is a fine doll, but maybe foreign to you, that's all." She gave me a thoughtful look, and then forced a smile. "That is your gift from Santa. Santa put it there to surprise you. Don't you like it?"

No, but I could not for some reason say it out loud. Nor did I pick her up.

Instead I had another question. If there are no trolls, then what about Santa? Was there a Santa?

"Santa came," mother said with conviction.

She led me to the nativity. A porcelain baby Jesus lay in his manger. Not only had Santa come, but baby Jesus had been born. I calmed down. My world started to right itself. And my new baby brother began to cry.

Father picked me up, I snuggled against his shoulder, and we all bundled in bed with the baby and my stocking full of goodies.

It was all right. We had a new baby, who was safe, and as for trolls, my parents never mentioned them ever again.

The Norwegian doll ended up in one of my dresser drawers buried under socks. For reasons I could not explain, I never gave her away. I even tried a few times to play with her; however, I always preferred playing with my little brother.

Mother finally quit asking me if I was ever going to name the doll. I never said so out loud, but for the rest of my childhood, I thought of her as the changeling.

Author's Note: *The Changeling* is the first in a series of immigrant short stories.

ABOUT the AUTHOR: KAREN FINNIGAN

Karen Finnigan is an editor and author of several historical romance novels. Originally from Seattle, she is a long-time resident of Idaho Falls. When not writing or reading, she enjoys her three grandchildren, dogs, cats, and gardening. Her novels, Harvest Song and Winter Song, are currently available on Amazon.

Please visit her website: Karenfinnigan.net.

Soup Can Labels and Red Wagons

by Daris Howard

My little three-year-old daughter, Celese, let go of my hand and rushed to the little red wagon. "Oh, Daddy. Can we get it for Christmas?! Can we?!"

I could see the longing in her smiling face and her sparkling eyes, but when I looked at the $60 price tag, my heart sank. As a college student, I was doing everything I could, but I was barely able to earn enough money for my family's needs. Besides teaching some classes and taking care of racehorses at nights and on Saturdays, I also did work at our apartment complex for half of our rent.

I knew Celese had dreamed of having a little wagon for her and her sister. A neighbor boy had one that he hauled all sorts of things around in, but he was not about to share it. Celese had seen a picture of one in a colored Sunday ad and had kept the ad in her room, sleeping with it under her pillow. I keenly felt her disappointment when I told her that we couldn't afford the wagon.

But then her face brightened again a moment later. "That's okay, Daddy. I will ask Santa for it."

Her heart was much lifted by the thought, but mine only felt heavier. Christmas was just over five weeks away, and I considered everything I could think of to get my little girl the present she so desperately wanted. I checked every second-hand store as well as all of the want ads, but there was no used wagon to be had.

Then my wife, Donna, showed me an ad in a woman's magazine. It had a picture of a red wagon, even nicer than the one Celese had asked for. It was normally $100, but a person could get it for free for 1000 soup can labels. She smiled. "If we could get 1000 soup can labels, we would only have to pay the $10 shipping."

I sighed. "Where am I going to get 1000 soup can labels? We can't afford canned soup."

She shrugged. "Well, it doesn't hurt to try. We could ask everyone we know to save them for us."

And that was what we did, and they all agreed to help us. Still, by the end of the week we only had 12 labels. I figured, at that rate, Celese would be married with children of her own before we'd have enough. But that night, as I took our garbage out to throw it into the dumpster, I saw something that gave me an idea. There, right on top, was a soup can. I found an old step stool and stood on it while I carefully sorted through the garbage. By the time I finished, I had 32 more labels.

When I brought them into our apartment, Donna mentioned that there were other apartment buildings that each had a dumpster. Grabbing my step stool, I went from one to the next, like a racoon rummaging for food. By the end of the night, I had collected dozens of labels. Each night after that, as soon as I arrived home from school and work, I went label hunting.

The deadline to have them mailed in was two weeks before Christmas, and the night before, I sat down to tally my collection. I was disappointed to find that I was 36 labels short. But, there was one apartment I never went to. It was about a quarter mile away, and the manager was a crotchety old man.

Everyone said he hated Christmas, and the youth in our community said he told them to leave when they came caroling. From what people told me about him, I figured I was likely to get shot if he found me going through his dumpster. But I was not about to get that close to my goal and still fail, so I grabbed the step stool and my small flashlight and headed to the dumpster of the man everyone had nicknamed Scrooge.

I quietly went about my work, digging through the dumpster, and had found 11 labels, when a loud voice sounded behind me. "What do you think you're doing?!"

I turned to face the bright beam of a huge flashlight. The old man everyone nicknamed Scrooge also held a baseball bat threateningly. It took all my courage to speak.

"I am gathering soup can labels."

He looked at me like he thought I had drunk fermented eggnog. "Why?"

I explained about my little daughter wanting a wagon, and how I was a college student and couldn't afford one. I then told him about the soup company promotion and how if I could get 1000 labels, I could get it for free. When I finished, I was sure he was going to call the police and have me arrested for trespassing. But instead, he asked, "How many do you have?"

"I have 964 at home, and I found 11 more here," I said, holding them up to show him.

He looked at me for a long time, and finally turned his flashlight from shining in my face. "You will be able to see better if you let me hold my big flashlight for you."

With his help, I eventually found another 19 labels. I still needed six more. When I finished, the old man swung his light around and commanded, "Come with me."

I followed him to his house. It looked like Christmas had skipped this little home. There was not a single Christmas decoration anywhere. He disappeared into the kitchen and came back with six cans of soup. He peeled off the labels and held them out to me. "Take these."

"But how will you remember what soup is in them?"

He shrugged, "Doesn't matter. Surprise soup is the best kind. Besides, at my age, they all taste the same."

I thanked him, and then he did something I didn't expect. He smiled and chuckled slightly. "You should have seen your face when I shown my flashlight on you. You've probably heard lots of scary stories about me, haven't you?"

I didn't know what to say, so I just shrugged and nodded as he continued. "Did you know I had a little girl once?"

I told him I didn't really know much about him. He shared with me how, one Christmas, his little girl had also wanted a wagon he couldn't afford, so he bought some lumber and made one. Tears welled up in his eyes as he finished. "The next year we lost her to the measles. She died on Christmas Day."

Suddenly, I understood more about this old man than most of the community ever knew, and I realized why he despised Christmas. We talked quite a while, and when I turned to leave, he asked me to wait. He retrieved an old ribbon and handed it to me. "Tell your little girls Santa sent it." He then smiled brightly. "Merry Christmas."

I thanked him and headed on my way. When I got home, I told Donna the story as we packaged the labels.

The next two weeks seemed long as we waited for the wagon. But on Christmas Eve, it arrived. I spent until 2:00 in the morning putting it together, placed the old ribbon on it, and set it under our small tree.

The sun wasn't even up the next morning when I heard Celese's squeals from the other room. "Annicka, he came! Santa came and he brought us a wagon!"

After breakfast was eaten and all the presents were unwrapped, it was time to go for a wagon ride. Everyone bundled up, and we tucked our two little girls into the wagon wrapped in a big blanket. I told them we had to go past Santa's house so he could see them in it.

When we got to Scrooge's home, Celese looked up at me. "Daddy, this couldn't be Santa's house. There are no Christmas decorations."

I just smiled and said maybe Santa was too busy to decorate. "Or," she considered, "maybe he isn't home yet from delivering presents."

We did see the old man standing in the window, and my girls waved. He smiled and waved back.

That night I took them in their wagon around to see the Christmas lights. When we passed Scrooge's house, we stopped. There was an old wreath on the door and an ancient set of lights glowing along the porch. Celese smiled. "Oh, look, Daddy. Santa must have come home."

"Yes, Sweetheart," I said. "I think he must have."

ABOUT the AUTHOR: DARIS HOWARD

Daris Howard is an author and playwright who grew up on a farm in rural Idaho. Throughout his life, he has associated with many colorful characters including cowboys, farmers, lumberjacks, truck drivers, factory workers, and others while working in these and other industries. He will jokingly say that his best job was working in a fast food establishment, because that was what gave him the motivation to attend college.

He was a state champion wrestler and competed in college athletics. He also lived for eighteen months in New York when he was 19 - 21 years old.

Daris and his wife, Donna, have ten children and were foster parents for several years. He has also worked in scouting and cub scouts, at one time having 18 boys in his scout troop. He is now a math professor and his classes are well known for the stories he tells to liven up discussion and to help bring across the points he is trying to teach.

His plays, musicals, and books build on the characters of those he has associated with, along with his many experiences. He also writes a popular weekly newspaper column called "Life's Outtakes" that are short stories from his life and the lives of those he has known. His scripts and books are much like his stories, full of humor and real life experiences.

He has had his plays translated into German and French and performed in many countries around the world. His plays have won many awards including the National Theatre Co-op Award, the Deseret Dramatic Award, semi-finalist in the Moondance Film and Theatre Festival, and his book, The Three Gifts, has won the Editor's Choice Award.

His books can be found at www.darishoward.com.

The Story of Santa's
Christmas Sack

by Daris Howard

Now and then one of my younger children will ask me how Santa fits all the toys in his sack. I tell them about a Christmas we had many years ago. It was a tough Christmas. We were a young married couple, going to college, with a brand-new baby. There was hardly enough money for the necessities, like rent, let alone the luxuries, like food.

Besides the tuition and the many other expenses, we were making payments to the hospital—we didn't want them to repossess our baby. Sometimes gas for our pickup could not even be purchased, and I found myself riding a bike the six miles to the university through the snow and cold, with bits of cardboard stuffed in the bottom of my shoes to help keep the water from coming through the holes in them.

Our major source of income came from any job I could find on the work board at the university, but it wasn't as constant as I would like nor were they high paying jobs. My wife and I made the decision that we could not afford Christmas presents, so, shortly after Thanksgiving, we took my five-month-old daughter's favorite toys and hid them so we could wrap them up and at least have something for her to open on Christmas.

Just before Christmas I was hired by a carpet cleaning company. I worked hard, but every dime that came in seemed to be eaten away by past bills. The discouragement of hard classes, little money for my family, and long hours at work began to settle on me like long, dark days at the North Pole.

To find my way out of this dismal time, I determined I would find some way to save some money, any money, to buy my wife something for Christmas. I would save my tips or any little extra I could, even though I was still forced to use it at times. As I finished up my last job on Christmas Eve, just before midnight, I counted my change and barely had five dollars.

I wanted her surprise to be something Christmassy, yet it needed to be practical, so I hurried to a grocery store that closed at midnight. When I was young, the only time I got oranges or nuts was at Christmas, and they still put me in the holiday mood, so I decided that would be the gift I'd give her. At ten cents a pound I bought a forty-pound box of oranges, about five pounds of nuts at the same price, and had enough left over for a candy bar.

I drove home with my surprise and left it all in my pickup. Our small apartment had one bedroom that wouldn't fit both a crib and a bed, so we slept on a lumpy hide-a-bed in the living room. When my wife went into the bedroom with our daughter, I raced outside and hauled the loot in and stuffed it in the coat closet.

About 2:00 in the morning, when my wife and daughter were asleep, I snuck into the bedroom to retrieve one of my wife's stockings. Now, in my defense, I must say that I grew up with almost all brothers and I knew very little about women or women's things, so in the dark, when I reached in her drawer and pulled out a nylon, I figured it was as good a stocking as any.

I stumbled my way back to the coat closet and started stuffing oranges into it as fast as I could. Every once in a while, I would reach into it to see if it was getting full, but the level of oranges never seemed to rise. At one point, my wife stirred and I was sure she was waking, so I quickly threw in my "I Love You Coupons", 3X5 cards with things I had written on them such as, "One I Love You Coupon Good For Breakfast In Bed" and things like that. I also threw in the nuts and the candy bar.

Her breathing leveled out again, so I started throwing in more oranges. But they were now noisily hitting the nuts and the cards. She sleepily asked what I was doing. "Nothing," I answered. "Go back to sleep." That doesn't work on Christmas morning and she rolled over and turned on the lamp by her bed.

There was her nylon, almost a full box of oranges in it, stretched wide enough you could wrap it around all the people from a third-world nation. She covered her mouth, trying not to laugh, but finally could contain herself no longer without choking and chortled gleefully as I blushed in embarrassment.

And that, I tell my children, is why Santa's sack will hold all of those toys. It is made out of nylon.

ABOUT the AUTHOR: DARIS HOWARD

Daris Howard is an author and playwright who grew up on a farm in rural Idaho. Throughout his life he has associated with many colorful characters including cowboys, farmers, lumberjacks, truck drivers, factory workers, and others while working in these and other industries. He will jokingly say that his best job was working in a fast food establishment, because that was what gave him the motivation to attend college.

SPINACH SALAD with POPPYSEED DRESSING

Submitted by Daris Howard

INGREDIENTS

- 1 bunch spinach
- 1 c. mandarin oranges
- walnuts with sugar glaze
- 3/4 lb. Sliced fresh mushrooms
- 1 head iceberg lettuce
- 3/4 c. grated swiss cheese
- 1 red onion, sliced
- ½ lb. Bacon cooked and crumbled
- ½ c. slivered almonds with 3 Tbsp. sugar, caramelized together
  Toss all ingredients together and make the dressing

POPPYSEED DRESSING
Mix together

- 3/4 Tbsp. poppy seeds
- 1/4 c. grated onion
- 1/3 c. white vinegar
- 3/4 tsp. salt
- 3/4 c. oil
- 1 Tbsp. prepared mustard
- 1/3 c. sugar

Casey's Tale

by Sandra Lord

FOR ADOPTION – MALE YORKIE-POO.

Yep, that's me--appearing on a computer screen on the desk opposite my cage. Let me tell you how it happened.

A nice person found me on the streets of Salem, Oregon, and brought me to this warm rescue shelter. It's so much better being here than trying to survive in the icy rain falling outside. One of the people here put my picture and a description of me on the shelter website.

I must admit the picture wasn't my best shot. I hardly recognized that scruffy-looking dog as myself. I doubt anyone would want me after seeing that picture.

After what seemed like forever in doggie time, a black thing on her desk rang. I poked my head between the bars and flipped my ear up to better hear what was going on. The lady was describing me to someone. When she stopped talking, she turned to me.

"Casey," that's the name she gave me, "a lady is coming here to see you. If your meeting turns out like I think it will, you'll be in your new home before Christmas."

I was happy hearing this news, yet scared at the same time. What would life throw at me now? So far, things haven't gone well, that is until I landed in this shelter.

Several hours later, which seemed forever to me, a woman walked into the room and approached my cage. She was a kind-looking human, but sadness showed in her eyes. Something told me she needed me as much as I needed her. Right then, I decided we had to have a future together.

Please, please let her feel the same.

She lifted me in her arms, and I saw tears in her eyes. I licked her cheek. That move did it. We bonded immediately.

Oh boy, things are looking good for me now.

After a short ride home, I landed in doggie heaven. I had a new bed, blanket, new dishes filled with food and water, and best of all—treats. I love treats and will do almost anything to get them. More important, I received lots of loving from Diane, my new mom. That's how I thought of this wonderful human. We played games—hide and seek and chase down the hall and around the breakfast bar in the kitchen. So much fun. I have a lot more games to teach Diane in the future.

For now, my main duty—without fail—is to protect mom from the two monsters residing in the house--a noisy washing machine that gives off a loud clunk when one least expects it and a big, black vacuum cleaner that roars and tries to suck everything up inside it. So far, my frenzied barking doesn't stop them. I suppose they think a ten-pound canine is no threat. But I try. I also answer the door bell, alerting Diane when a stranger is outside. You see, I'm a very smart dog, so my mom and her friends tell me. I constantly look out the living room window on guard duty to see who dares to approach our house. I don't bark when I know who is out there. Instead, I jump up in Diane's arms (to better see) and greet her friend.

On one of our morning walks around the neighborhood, I met Ace, the large Standard Poodle who lives next door to Diane. He's nice for a big dog. After sniffs and tail wagging, he told me Diane was recently widowed and is very lonely.

Yeah, I know. We dogs can only do so much.

Still, we put our heads together, quite a feat between a tall and short dog. We concentrated on various ways to make her happier, especially during this holiday season. Not a good time to be alone. Christmas is rapidly approaching. We have to do something fast.

I glanced over to the gazebo across the street and saw Craig walking Oscar, his Basset Hound. Now, I don't care much for Oscar. He scares me with his deep bark, though I don't let him know that. He's big, must weigh a ton, at least that's my impression looking from the ground up. Goodness, even just one of his large, droopy ears is bigger than me.

But you see, Craig is also lonely having lost his partner a year ago. I turned to Ace.

"Maybe we should get Craig and Diane together as friends to attend some of the events coming up. They could go to the beach, see a movie or play, eat out at the many restaurants close by - so many things to do here in this area. I'll even make the effort to befriend Oscar."

Ace reminded me the Nutcracker Suite was playing at the Community Center. This could be the beginning to bring these two humans together. Ace said he would grab the brochure of the play from his house and put it on Craig's porch, which he did that afternoon. I'm not sure how he accomplished that feat, probably carried it in his teeth. Ace is almost as smart as me.

On my evening walk with Diane, I saw many of the homes had their Christmas lights on. I tugged on my leash, which I do quite frequently, pulling Diane across the street to where Craig and Oscar were walking. I managed to be on my good behavior toward Oscar, a great strain for me. The effort was worth it seeing how well the two humans got along.

Whoopee—it worked! I'm so proud of Ace and myself. Craig and Diane had a great time seeing the play. Amazing what a smart dog can do. I'm happy mom is getting out and meeting new people.

I know I'm the center of her new life, as she is mine. Still, she also needs new friends. Oh yes, everything is going to plan.

It's the day before Christmas. The house is decorated and baking smells are rolling out of the kitchen. Craig is coming over tomorrow for Christmas day dinner. I see lots of presents under the tree with my name on them. *Yes, I can read.* I'm so spoiled and love every minute of it.

Being in the Christmas spirit, I wish my new friends here in the neighborhood a Merry Christmas. I pray all dogs in need find a good home like I did in the coming New Year.

Oh yeah, I better include *cats* in my Christmas Wish. Diane's sister has two of the beasts.

ABOUT the AUTHOR: SANDRA LORD

Sandra Lord's desire to write goes back to her early years, growing up in Spokane and Chelan, Washington. Years later, she graduated with a B.A. degree from Washington State University in Pullman, Washington. After college, she worked the next thirty years as a technical writer/editor in the nuclear industry. She is published in nonfiction (newspaper and newsletter articles) and co-authored several technical reports at the Idaho National Engineering Laboratory (INEL). She is married to Bill Yarbrough, a retired Lt. Colonel from the Air Force Reserve and retired nuclear engineering physicist from the INEL. Sandra is a charter member of Blue Sage Writers, located in Idaho Falls, Idaho.

Her love of animals led her to write Casey's Tale, a detour from her regular writing genre. Sandra is published in military romantic suspense. Her novel, Wings of Fate, takes place in the latter days of the Cold War. The crash of a top-secret Looking Glass aircraft in the North Cascades of Washington State brings together two former lovers in the efforts to recover the classified equipment on board.

Go to Sandra's website, www.sandralord.net or Amazon for more information.

The Streets of Bethlehem

by Maxine McCoy

At night Jotham roamed the streets in the humble town of Bethlehem. Tonight, would be no different. Yet, a strange feeling in his chest, so strong that it made his breath catch and his scalp tingle, told him the night would be momentous.

He had a gift. He sensed things before they happened, perceived the feelings of others, and sometimes could even read their thoughts. Mother told him to keep it to himself. There were some who wouldn't appreciate that such a special gift had been bestowed upon the illegitimate son of a servant woman.

He lived in the house of Timotheus, a family dwelling that gave shelter to three generations. His mother had cooked the evening meal in the open court. He could hear her there, cleaning up. The family had gone up on the roof to sit and talk about the day, as they did most evenings. They'd taken their bedding with them, so he knew they planned to sleep there.

The animals came into the house at night to a room designated for that purpose. One of Jotham's jobs was to herd them in. His master was a tent maker and the young man assisted him during the day, running errands, gathering tools, and cutting the rough goat's hair cloth.

As he prepared to take his bedding to the roof, Thaddeus, the master's son, approached. "Why are you not working, slave?"

"I finished what I was told to do." He hated the quiver in his voice.

"Then wash my feet. I seem to have gotten them dusty." The young master smirked and looked at his two friends for approval.

Jotham found a towel and filled a basin with water. When he knelt to perform his task, Thaddeus kicked the container over, spilling its contents.

"Look what you've done, you clumsy fool." The boy slapped the servant's face.

"I didn't . . .."

Thaddeus hit him again. "How dare you talk back to me."

The other boys knocked Jotham down, taunting and laughing. He could beat any one of them in a fair fight, but he mustn't. He was a slave. Not only would it bring punishment to himself, but to his mother. So, he bit his tongue until he tasted blood, and willed his tears not to flow.

While he cleaned up the water, the boys grew tired of their bullying and wandered off. He took his bedding to the roof. The cool air soothed the heat on his face that boiled from within. He moved past the others and settled in a far corner at the other end, well away from the family.

As soon as it was quiet, except for the snoring of old grandmother, he slipped off the side of the wall and climbed down the vines into the central court. Stepping outside, he took a deep breath of freedom. Now he could go where he wanted, do what he desired. He owned the night; the darkness was his home.

He ran toward the marketplace, his bare feet silent on the dusty road. The ancient city sat tall on a commanding ridge, though it had diminished in size and importance since King David had been born there. It was said by those of old that Jacob had buried Rachel near its gate. Ruth had come here with Naomi to call it home. The town sat above a natural aquafer, lending it all the water it needed for the terraced hills, the surrounding fields of grain, the fig, olive, and almond trees that grew in abundance.

Here, shepherds watched over their sheep in the fields, venders sold their wares in town, carpenters made their tables, stools, and chests, and tentmakers crafted homes for wanderers. The farmers grew their grain and bound their sheaves. It seemed that everyone had a place in this society but a lowly slave boy

He turned a corner and stopped. The marketplace was quiet and empty now. Earlier today, he'd been sent to buy heavy thread. The noise of a hundred voices had filled the air. Children played in the street; beggars beseeched passersby for money; venders touted their wares. The sick, and lame sat against the buildings and watched the people go by. It had been even more crowded than usual because of the Jews that had come from other towns to pay their taxes.

It was here that he'd seen the woman. She rode a donkey, hunched forward, clutching at her stomach, her face drawn up in pain. She was heavy with child. A tall, bearded man led the animal, looking back often, his features etched with anxiety. Jotham had walked with them, staying slightly behind so they wouldn't notice, filled with an emotion he could only describe as joy. Why would his heart swell with happiness at such a time of distress?

Tonight, something seemed off. The place didn't seem as glorious. A shadow crept across the whitewashed stucco wall of the building next to him. There were dangerous gangs of robbers who lurked about at night. He sensed that they were near. He had to be careful that they didn't see him. Stepping into the shadows, he took a deep breath and held it.

Waiting.

Maybe he'd imagined the menacing impression. Cautiously, he moved from shadow to shadow, looking back over his shoulder often. He saw no one, but he couldn't rid himself of the feeling that someone watched. He began to run, looking back.

Smack!

He rammed into something hard and dropped to the ground.

A short, bearded man with a powerful chest lunged toward him, stepped on his neck, and pressed down. The stranger glared at the stunned boy. "What are you doing here?"

With the foot on his throat, Jotham had to struggle to say the words. "I'm just

. . .wandering . . . around."

The foot pressed harder. "You lie. Who sent you?"

"No one. I swear . . . by a thousand camels. I sneak out. . . at night . . . without my mother knowing." Four more faces appeared above him.

"What shall we do?" one of the them asked.

The pressure on Jotham's throat eased. "If I let you go, will you tell no one you saw us?"

"Yes, I promise."

"If you're lying, I'll find you."

The thieves walked away laughing.

"I can tell by what he wore that he's only a slave, and a puny one at that. Probably wouldn't sell for much," one of them said. "You scared him so bad, he'll never sneak out again."

Jotham gritted his teeth. Obviously, they didn't know him. When they were down the street a few yards, he followed, straining to listen as their voices grew quieter and more cautious.

"What did the travelers say?" asked the leader.

"They said to meet them at the sun dial."

Jotham was curious, but he didn't have to follow. He knew where the sun dial was. He crept through town on the outer streets, doubled back to the center of the square, and hid behind a cart. The robbers hovered in the shadows near the sun dial, two of them pacing, the other three standing rigidly still.

They didn't have long to wait. Two sun-darkened foreigners hurried intro the square, looking back over their shoulders.

"Were you followed," one of five asked.

"No," the tallest traveler said. "We aren't stupid."

Another of the five thieves held out something that Jotham couldn't see. "This is worth more than its weight in gold. We stole it from a caravan coming from the east."

Jotham lost interest in the transaction. What caught his eye instead, was the sun dial. It glowed more at this moment than it had when the sun shone on it in midday.

"It's time." He felt the words rather than heard them.

His heart drummed against his ribs. Hands began to tingle. Elation caused him to forget his need to hide. He caught his breath and stepped forward to stare at the sun dial.

"Who's that?" one of the strangers yelled.

A robber pointed his finger. "It's that slave boy. I told you we should have gotten rid of him." The man who spoke leaped forward.

Jotham ran.

He swerved in and out of houses, around deserted carts, and through courtyards. The man chased him, staying close behind. Frightened, Jotham headed for the outskirts of town. He ran until his breath burned through his chest; rocks pierced his bare feet.

When he left the town and entered a field, the man who pursued him gave up and turned back. Jotham continued to run straight through a herd of sheep until his legs dropped from under him. The animals crowded around, bleating and turning in circles.

Shepherds stood nearby. Each wore a tunic, and over that a mantle made of sheepskin, with the fleece turned inward. Their heads were wrapped in roughly woven woolen cloth. A bright light shone down on them. Oblivious to the exhausted boy, they stared into the sky, fear in their eyes, their mouths dropped open in surprise. Jotham crawled closer.

A quiet voice slipped into his mind. "Blessed are you, Jotham, for what you are about to behold."

In the center of the light stood a man clothed in white, his feet several inches above the ground. "For unto you is born this day in the city of David a Savior, who is Christ the Lord. And this shall be a sign unto you; ye shall find the Babe wrapped in swaddling clothes, lying in a manger." When the messenger spoke, his powerful voice filled the boy with unspeakable joy.

Other spirits appeared in the heavens, singing, "Glory to God in the highest, and on earth peace, good will toward men."

Jotham stood among the sheep gaping up at the display above him. When the singing ended, the angels disappeared, and the light dissipated. The field grew dark and the stars seemed to shine more brightly than before. The shepherd that recovered first said, his voice filled with awe, "Let us go into Bethlehem and see what the Lord hath made known to us."

They argued briefly over who should stay with the sheep, then all of them strode across the field, none wanting to be left behind. Jotham went too. He did not doubt who the parents of the magnificent babe would be.

The shepherds had no trouble finding the manger. There, in the little cave nestled against the hill, sat the woman on a pile of hay, looking tired but radiant. A soft smile curved across her beautiful face. Her husband stood close by, gazing down at her with love. In a feeding trough filled with straw, lay the baby, wrapped in soft blankets. He slept soundly, sucking on two tiny fingers.

The young slave entered quietly and sat by the door unnoticed. He had come to worship the Savior of the world. The Babe was the son of God. Heavenly Father loved His children so much that He sent His Son to save them from their sins, as the holy ones had prophesied.

All Jotham's inferior feelings, the hurt, the sadness, the fear, melted away. It all became clear to the humble servant. He had been allowed to witness a miracle. God loved him. Even an illegitimate son of a poor servant woman.

ABOUT THE AUTHOR: MAXINE MCCOY

The character for Maxine's next book resides in the space between thought and word.

Maxine has traveled to every state in the United States and five other countries. She has lived in six different states and many cities. Along the way, she fostered a love for people—their customs and folkways, their fortunes and follies.

As an Anthropologist, Maxine developed a deep respect for the Native American people and their cultures. When she worked as a counselor in the criminal justice system, she learned how truly complex individuals can be. As a Genealogist, she researches her ancestors, and studies their lives and histories.

These interests flavor her fictional adventures. The psychological dimensions of her characters, the backgrounds furnished by places she's known and loved, and the yesterdays of her heritage all come together as material for her stories.

Maxine currently resides in southeastern Idaho with her tiny Yorkie, Sassy, who lives up to her name.

Maxine has a new novel, THE TARNISHED MOON, available on Amazon and on her author website: maxinemccoy.com

BACON WRAPPED CHICKEN

submitted by Maxine McCoy

INGREDIENTS

- 6 boneless skinless chicken breast halves
- 8 ounces cream cheese with onions and chives
- 1 tablespoon butter, cubed
- 6 bacon strips

INSTRUCTIONS

Flatten chicken* to ½ inch thickness. Spread 3 tablespoons cream cheese over each. Dot with butter and sprinkle with salt; roll up. Wrap each with a bacon strip. Place seam side down, in a greased 13 inch X 9 inch X 2 inch baking pan. Bake uncovered at 400 degrees for 30 – 40 minutes or until juices run clear. Broil 6 inches from the heat for 5 minutes or until bacon is crisp. Yield – 6 servings.

*Flattening the chicken: Place one chicken breast between two pieces of waxed paper. Starting in the center and working to the edges, pound lightly with the flat side of a meat mallet until the chicken is even in thickness.

The Miracle at Midnight

by Peggy Nelson

It was a cold and snowy Christmas Eve, but it was warm and cozy inside the little cottage where Serena and her mom lived. Although the cottage was in town, it was nestled among trees at the end of a long driveway, which made it a wonderland unto itself.

Serena was three years old and full of unrepressed joy at the anticipation of Santa's arrival. Although she had few memories of other Christmases, her mama and grandparents had shown her baby photos of when she was on Santa's lap.

Mama had tucked Serena in bed that night and cradled her little face, brushing back the unruly curls and kissing her on both cheeks while she snuggled her close and read her one last story.

"Tonight will be a magic night, my love. The Christmas tree is lit and the cookies are on the mantle for when Santa arrives. You must sleep tight and dream of sugar plums, just like the poem we read tonight."

Serena's eyes were bright with anticipation, but as her mama softly sang to her, they grew heavy. Soon she fell into a deep sleep and dreamed of all the wonders that awaited her on Christmas morning.

Sometime during the dark night, Serena awoke. She opened her eyes and looked around. Her room was illuminated by a night light and the glow from the moon and the snow-covered ground outside, and she could hear her mama's soft snoring in the adjoining room. She hugged her dolly close to her and closed her eyes, but the image of the wonders below enticed her to get up.

Serena was a tiny, but careful girl. She tiptoed down the stairs and sat at the foot of the Christmas tree, enchanted by the lights and the beautiful array of ornaments. Her favorite was a spritely elf who wore green boots and a candy-striped red and green jacket with red tights. "Hello little elf," Serena whispered.

"Well, hello little girl," said the elf, bouncing up and down. "Would you like to join our party?"

One by one, the angels, fairies, and bouncy puppies all began jingling and jangling, urging her to join them.

"But I'm too big – I don't fit on the tree," Serena lamented with tears in her beautiful brown eyes. She really wanted to join them.

"Ah, my little friend," said the elf, "all it takes is a wee bit of magic!" With that, he sprang from the tree limb and landed on her leg. "Abracadabra fiddle dee dee, you can join us up on the tree!" The elf jumped to her head, did a quick jig and Serena flew up among the other ornaments, trailing fairy dust. Magically, she had sprouted a pair of gossamer wings and her flannel pajamas had turned into a silky yellow dress, soft as a flower. She was beautiful with her golden curls and ever-changing expressions of wonder.

"I can fly!" Serena exclaimed as she flitted from branch to branch, dancing briefly with each of the ornaments. The elf chortled with mischievous glee, the puppies yipped, and the perfect angels opened their wings to welcome her. Everything was magic - that is, until the sound of hooves on the roof and snow sprinkling down the chimney startled all of her friends into silence.

"Quickly Serena," cried the elf, "fly up the stairs and into bed – I'll follow you and work my magic in reverse!" Up she flew. Serena was so tiny that she barely made a wrinkle in the coverlet. The elf rapidly invoked his charm reversal, "Abracadabra back to bed, back to the little girl I once led." The elf leapt up and planted a kiss on the tip of her nose. Serena fell sound asleep with visions of flight propelling her through a dreamy landscape.

"Sweetheart, wake up," Serena's mom once again cradled her head and kissed her cheeks. "it's morning and I do believe that Santa came while we were sleeping!"

Serena's eyes popped open and she hugged her mom. "Are the elves and angels and puppies still having a party?"

Her mom looked at her quizzically. "I think you are still dreaming my tiny love. Come on, let's go downstairs." With that, her mom scooped her out of bed and carried her down to the living room. Serena could smell her mom's coffee and the sweetness of cinnamon rolls in the oven. There was fresh snow scattered on the rug by the hearth, and the cookies they left out the night before were gone.

"Christmas . . . "Serena sighed deeply as she looked at the many gifts under the tree, especially the red wagon that Santa had left for her. It held a big teddy bear and a stuffed unicorn. Her eyes were bright as she sat cross-legged next to the wagon. Her mom sat and cuddled with her – both of their eyes shining with the wonder of it all.

The sun was beginning to rise as Serena looked up at her friends in the glittering tree. *It had felt so real – was it only a dream?* She wiggled her shoulders, hoping that wings would appear, but sadly, they didn't. She could no longer fly.

Serena looked up at the beautiful tree and found her favorite elf. He was on one of the highest branches. "Hi Elf," she whispered. He jingled only slightly, as if a small breeze had moved him. But then Serena saw him smile and wink for just a second, and she knew her dream had been real.

ABOUT the AUTHOR: PEGGY NELSON

Peggy Nelson was born and raised in Seattle, Washington. She taught English for many years at Eastern Idaho Technical College, now College of Eastern Idaho, retiring in 2017 after 30 years in Education and Industry.

Peggy's novel, "Ash Tuesday," a work of speculative fiction, was written collaboratively with her sister and niece. It is available through Amazon.

GOLDEN SAUCE

INGREDIENTS
- 1 cup sugar
- 1/2 cup butter
- 3 egg yolks
- 1 cup of whipped whipping cream

INSTRUCTIONS
- Beat yolks until thick, then gradually beat in the sugar.
- Cook until mixture coats a metal spoon, then remove from heat.
- Chill thoroughly
- Fold in firmly whipped cream.
- Flavor lightly with vanilla
- Chill before serving.

My husband's grandmother brought this recipe from Wales and in the years his mother hosted Thanksgiving, she always made this to go along with "carrot pudding", another Welsh dish. However, it is so delicious that we would use it for pumpkin pie and sometimes straight out of a little bowl. She always had to triple the recipe!

Sahara Solstice

by Phillip Nolte

Though it was only 0630, and the orangish star in the bright, cloudless, purple sky was barely above the horizon, conditions on the surface of the far-off planet were already dangerously hot. Dr. Alton Bradley made his way across the dry, dusty compound between the sleeping quarters on his spaceship and his two-room laboratory, which was a human-manufactured prefab module.

Another day that was going to be a real scorcher.

"They warned you about the solstice on this planet, Bradley," he said, "and now it's only a couple days away." He'd been talking to himself more and more lately, probably because he was the only human on planet Piscis Austrini II, dubbed "New Sahara" by the team who discovered it some five years earlier. Even in the high temperate latitudes, where he currently was, conditions on the planet were hot enough to be unsuitable for human habitation.

Not that the last part really mattered. Bradley wasn't a colonist, he was a scientist and, he supposed, an ambassador of sorts. The planet was sparsely populated by native beings who called themselves Agogwe, which literally translated meant simply "Those Who Endure." The Agogwe were mammalian, similar to the primates of Old Earth, but different enough that the xenobiologists decided to create a separate taxonomic branch for them. They were bipedal, about three feet tall on average, and had long, naked prehensile tails. To aid in dissipating the oppressive heat, their leathery, buff-colored skin was practically hairless, and their expandable, outsized ears were paper-thin and heavily-veined. Their large, luminous eyes (New Sahara got very dark at night) were a deep violet color.

The biologists said the little creatures were intelligent, nearly on par with humans, but their civilization was in its infancy and highly unlikely to advance very much further. The race was dying out, and Bradley could do nothing about it. He was prohibited from interfering with "the natural development of primitive species" by United Federation of Planets decree. In order to learn something of Agogwe society and culture before they became extinct, High Command reluctantly allowed a single human—him—to land on the surface and live among the natives for three months to observe and collect information.

He'd landed two and a half months ago and was eagerly accepted by the little natives.

"Where will I find the strength to leave these bright and gentle creatures to their fate?" he thought, as he slipped through the laboratory entry portal. The question had nagged him since his arrival, and he became ever more depressed about it as his departure date approached.

Though the temperature inside the module was above 80 F, it still felt blessedly cool, and he experienced a wave of relief as a blast of cooler air washed over him. He drew up short at his workstation and frowned. His computer was booted up. He knew he'd logged off before leaving last night and though the security wasn't airtight, it should have been adequate. He looked around and spotted L'Naar, shaman of the Agogwe village, across the chamber at the module's beverage dispenser.

"Would you like some coffee, Dr. Bradley?"

To make the best use of his short stay, Bradley had taught L'Naar to speak and read Human Standard language using the survey ship's neural-direct teaching console. It was a minor infraction of Federation policy, but one he deemed necessary given the utter lack of time.

"Thanks, L'Naar," he said as he accepted the coffee. "Um... did you access my computer?"

"I did, Dr. Bradley." The ready admission came as no surprise, deception was a foreign concept to the natives. To his knowledge, they'd never been anything but truthful.

"How did you get past the security?"

"Agogwe hearing is very sensitive. I could not help but overhear as you stroked the control panel. I duplicated the sounds and was granted access. "

"You shouldn't have done that."

The little alien was silent for a moment. "My sincere apologies, Dr. Bradley. You did not say it was forbidden."

Bradley thought for a moment and realized he hadn't expressly told L'Naar the computer was off-limits. That had been an oversight. At that moment, it occurred to him there was a pretty good chance the xenobiologists had grossly underestimated Agogwe intelligence.

What was important now was damage control.

"What is it you're looking for?" asked Bradley.

"Information about human technology."

"I'm not allowed to show you any of that, L'Naar."

Another short silence. "Why?"

"My government forbids me to interfere with the natural development of your people."

L'Naar shook his head in a very human manner. "The need for your technology is urgent, Dr. Bradley. Our planet becomes more uninhabitable by the day. Over the last twenty cycles, our population has declined dangerously. Soon there will be none of us left to 'develop naturally' as you put it.

"Not only that, you have already altered our 'natural development' by merely being here. Does 'not interfering' mean you would allow us to die out because the technology to improve conditions for us will 'contaminate' us? My people are running out of time, Doctor. I only seek to find ways for us to survive. Your people and your technology have given us hope. Would you now take that away from us?"

Bradley was torn between the rigors of duty and the compulsion to help these gentle creatures. At that moment, he was struck with a flash of insight. The decree forbid interference with "natural development," but contained no guidelines regarding "extinction." His spirit soared as the solution to this dilemma became obvious. His superiors might take exception, but as the only human on the entire planet, he had authority to act on behalf of all Mankind. Knowing he was doing the right thing, he beckoned his alien friend over to the computer. "Come, I'll show you how to do this."

Two days later, in the searing heat of the solstice, Bradley again made his way over to the laboratory. He leaned against the wall inside the entry portal, savoring the cool air inside. Since deciding to do everything possible to save the Agogwe, he had exposed the rest of the villagers to his neural-direct teaching machine and provided L'Naar and his people full access to the vast store of human knowledge contained in the lab computer's library. L'Naar wasn't at the terminal as he had been the last two mornings, but three of the other natives were gathered around it.

"Ah, Dr. Bradley, we've been waiting for you," called L'Naar from across the lab. "Please, follow me." He disappeared into the second chamber. Intrigued, Bradley followed.

In the center of the chamber was one of the hardy native bushes bedecked with colorful fruits and handcrafted bits of Agogwe art.

"What's all this?"

"During our studies, we discovered humans have a ritual of renewal that coincides with the solstice. You call it 'Christmas,' I believe."

Bradley was without words as the significance of what was before him hit home.

"You've given us a future when we thought all was lost, Dr. Bradley. It will be an honor to observe this special occasion with you."

MERRY CHRISTMAS!

ABOUT the AUTHOR: PHILLIP NOLTE

I am a potato scientist (yes, there are a few of us) who was transplanted from Minnesota to Idaho in 1991. I started writing science fiction in the mid nineteen eighties and recently (2012) turned my hand to writing novels. Since then I've produced the "Junkyard Dogs Trilogy" and the "Guardians of the Galactic Sentinel" series. A number of my short stories are collected under one cover in "Cannibals Shrink Elvis' Head." "Sahara Solstice" was prepared especially for this collection and, as you can see, I decided to stick with the genre most familiar to me: science fiction. My other books can be found at www.phillipnolte.com.

ROSIE'S ROCKY ROAD BARS

INGREDIENTS

- 1 12oz bag semi-sweet chocolate morsels
- 1 12oz bag butterscotch morsels
- 1 cup peanut butter
- 1/2 cup butter
- 1 package miniature marshmallows
- 1 lb. Spanish peanuts OR mixed nuts, walnuts, etc.

Melt butter, peanut butter and chips in double boiler. Cool slightly and add peanuts and marshmallows. Spread in greased 9 X 12" pan. Cool, cut into bars and serve.

Death is but a Shadow

by Charm O'Ryan

A Christmastime Miracle of a Different Sort

Christmas…

The very word spreads warmth inside those who speak of, or hear, it. It rebirths the spirit of selfless giving of time, gift, and deed. It brings forth memories of sacrifice, unconditional love, and precious family togetherness found in both church and home. Songs about snow, reindeer, Santa, Christmas trees, and praise to the Highest radiate from phones, radios, televisions, department store speakers.

Christmas…

The very word creates inner joy at the site of wide-eyed children caught up in the magic of believing in something greater than the human eye can see. It has the ability to recall the scent of pine trees and chimney smoke wafting in the air; of fresh-baked cinnamon rolls, steaming hot chocolate, tasty peppermint teas and candies, pies, roast beef, and other delicious foods prepared for the traditional holiday feast.

Christmas…

The very word instills a spirit of thankfulness; the deep appreciation of all one has been given throughout life past to present: health, peace, contentment, genuine happiness, and a financial-security comfortability that chases away fears of not having enough.

But for some?

Christmas…

The very word is a precursor to unfathomable loneliness; a tragic reminder of a loved one's absence from a person's once perfect world; a loved one no longer walking the face of this earth, no longer able to be held or kissed, no longer able to answer the phone when called with a number memorized over an entire lifetime by those left behind.

Christmas…

The very word births stress for those unable to provide for family members who anxiously await the goodies they anticipate and just might rightly deserve. Suicidal thoughts flow like rivulets of melting snow alongside barren streets, gushing toward rusty drainage gates; hopelessness replaces hope as another precious life is lost in a cycle of deep despair on, or around, what many have called the most wonderful time of the year.

Death is but a Shadow is a short story based on the supernatural experience I shared with my grandmother, Hazel Mildred Juanita Clark Silva, as she lay dying of a rare form of Vasculitis. The date was December 9th, 1996, and although it was one of the saddest days of my life, it was also one of the most important. Why? Because my grandmother, who I was especially close to, taught me how to shed mortality by revealing secrets about the entire dying process: sickness, death, and the surreal journey to life again.

Let me back up a little. When my grandma had a stroke-like experience, I flew to Boise, Idaho on November 9th, 1996, to be with her and my mama. I carried an animated Mrs. Clause doll and a boxed waltzing couple Christmas music scene, gifts for *Granny Goose* as she was known by her grandchildren, in my arms during the short flight. When I arrived at the hospital, grandma was still unresponsive. My mama was sitting in the corner and told me there had been no change…she hadn't gained consciousness in the 48 hours she'd been there.

Setting my gifts aside, I stepped to her bedside, and took hold of her hand. "Grandma, it's me, Charmie. I came to see you."

Aged eyelids fluttered before opening. The creamy glaze of death still covered the sparkling blue shine I was accustomed to seeing. "Hi, my beautiful Grandma. I flew on a plane just to come be with you."

I felt fingers squeeze mine as the true-blue shade of the eyes I loved and knew became more visible, the creamy film disappearing with each passing second.

"You...sweet...little...thing," she whispered, each hoarse word pronounced slow, each formed between lips that struggled to obey grandma's silent command to move.

These were the first words she had said in over two days and I was thrilled she had awakened to my voice.

I spent about ten days with her, my parents, aunts, uncles, and several cousins. During that time, *Goose* had most of us in stitches; she told us she was a '*lay-down*' rather than a '*stand-up*' comedian and she had returned just to make us laugh. Whether it was the telling of clean often corny jokes, the strange, little, off-the-wall comments she'd blurt out, or the *deep* appreciation for the endless parade of good-looking men that dared to enter her room under the guise of doctors, nurses, and therapists, she had us smiling, chuckling, and sometimes wanting to duck under our chairs! God forbid one of the male staffers should bend down. Or turn their back. In those instances, the family was privy to the batting of long eyelashes, the tilting of her hoary head to rest on a frail raised shoulder, and the appearance of teeth, biting the air as though she wanted to eat the handsome man who had entered her lair. By the time they stood, or turned around, her countenance had returned to its normal self: stoic and extremely interested in what it was they were saying.

111

Oh, yes. She was quite the character.

Like all good things, however, the bad tends to hover nearby; there's always an opposite.

At night and at times throughout the day grandma's fever would spike. Or she'd have episodes where she just didn't feel good. Doctors ran test after test that produced more questions than answers. They'd shake their heads and admit they were perplexed. Each new day challenged their expertise as continued testing and lab work ruled out their current suspicions and stifled their morning declarations of "It's possible that it's—." Try as they may, they couldn't give us a concrete diagnosis. They couldn't pinpoint the cause of her declining health.

I spent most of the ten days beside her, only leaving to eat and/or smoke a quick cigarette outside. The entire family took turns spending the night with her, so she'd never be without one of us nearby.

Throughout grandma's bedridden days, especially her sicker times, I was privy to her dip into the spiritual realm and was the only one in the room when the first *unseen visitor* made an appearance. At first, I thought she was seeing an angel…an angel who had come to take her to an eternal home.

Tears filled my eyes. "Describe her to me."

"You can't see her?" She stared at the wall to her right.

"No, Grandma, I can't."

"She's a plain woman, no makeup, her hair twisted up in a Pentecostal bun. She's wearing a grey high-necked dress."

"What's she doing?"

"Just sitting there, staring at me." She cocked her head to one side. "I see common people on the streets behind her."

"What are they doing?"

"Milling around, going about their business, I guess. Oh—she's gone now."

I was never more relieved than when the woman left.

She wasn't an angel.

She hadn't taken grandma anywhere.

That incident was the first of several ethereal entities to come to grandma's room. And, usually, I found myself the receiver of their well-described yet *invisible* presence. Other than a little blonde-haired boy who showed up at her bedside when my cousin, Sherry, was spending the night in her room, I was present for *all* of her unique guests.

Other family members were in the room with me when six of her seven aunts came to stand at the foot of her bed. *Goose* called out their names as she introduced them to us. They had prepared a feast and spread it out before her. We watched her grab food we could *not* see, take bites, chew, and swallow it down. She even ate corn on the cob from one side to the other and told us how wonderful everything tasted.

Yes, it was stranger than fiction to see grandma relish the tasty meal and enjoy the company of her aunts, evidenced by the asking and answering of questions we could *not* hear. And I can understand how some of you who are reading about this experience might think a high fever caused such a grand hallucination. But for those of us present? We didn't believe that was the case. Especially, when coupled with what we discovered later. One of grandma's aunts, Aunt Molly, was still very much alive at that time. Such factual knowledge made perfect sense as to *why* she was not present with the other six.

Even the little boy had a possible explanation of who he might have been. Grandma had suffered a miscarriage years after the live births of two girls and a boy.

Looking back, I believe my grandmother hovered between two worlds: the natural and the supernatural. I believe this is why she could *see* and *hear* what we could not. To offer proof, I can site two examples. One, my auntie, returning from the hospital cafeteria, saw her dressed in a beautiful wedding gown, twirling and dancing in one of the hospital corridors two floors below her room. Little did Auntie know that her sister, my mama, was upstairs telling grandma it was okay to leave...she could go dance with grandpa...we'd all be okay.

And, two, probably the most evidential piece of proof I can offer, was the *Lady In Red*.

My mother and auntie, both in their sixties back then, were exhausted and needed a break from the hospital so they could bathe and get some much-needed sleep. Grandma was annoyed about something, but they weren't sure what. Thinking it was their wanting to leave that had soured her mood, they promised to return.

"We'll be back, Mama," Auntie whispered.

"In the morning," my mother added.

"No hurry, my darlings. Get some rest."

Gathering up their things, they kissed her goodbye and headed for the door. Auntie's hand on the doorknob, grandma's voice gave her pause.

"Be sure to tell that lady in red to shut up. She's loud, obnoxious, and just plain rude to be so boisterous."

Her two daughters exchanged glances. "What lady?" they asked in unison.

"The one in red," she reiterated. "You can't miss her. She's the loud one!"

With a nod, they left the room. They walked down one hall and turned left. Then down another and took a right. Veering around another corner, they could hear a woman's booming voice as she came into view.

They froze.

A woman dressed in a red dress with a red scarf wrapped around her neck was leaning over the nurses' counter, talking to a male and female nurse. Laughter tipped back her head and they noticed the fire-engine-red lipstick smeared across both lips. Red, high-heeled, open-toed shoes exposed red toenail polish which was an exact match to the red polish covering her long fake fingernails.

Mouths agape, my mother and auntie continued to the elevator and pushed the button. Grandma had not been out of bed in days, and there was no possible way she had seen the woman from her room.

Most, definitely, grandma's spirit was *not* staying in her body one-hundred-percent of the time.

On the ninth day I was there, it was optimistically and unanimously decided *Goose* would move in with my auntie whenever she was released from the hospital. I volunteered to stay with my grandmother so my mama & auntie and a few helpful cousins could go pack up and clean out her tiny retirement apartment.

Grandma napped off and on throughout the day. When she'd wake, she'd often stare out the window across the room from her hospital bed where several chairs sat beneath the mock-marbled window ledge. It was late afternoon when the mysterious fever returned.

"What'd you say, Bebby?" she whispered, her voice groggy with either sleep or the rise of internal temperature.

Recognizing her pet name for my mother, Betty, I responded. "Mama's not here, Grandma. She went to your apartment, remember?"

"Oh, that's right." Her gaze settled on the one chair kiddy-cornered to the side of the window. "I don't just hear her, you know, I see her—her too." Several small coughs worked to clear the crackled-sounding mucus rising from inside her throat. Conquering the battle, but not the war, she whispered, "Can you hand me my water, Honey?"

With a nod, I grabbed the mug off the bedside table, and held the accordion straw to her lips. She drew water inside her mouth, swished it around, and swallowed. We chitchatted for a moment before Grandma's eyelids lowered once more.

Before I could return to my own seat, they snapped back open.

"That's okay, Beppy. I love you too." She armed several wayward curls off her brow as her gaze roamed the empty chairs. "Still not there, huh?"

I shook my head from side to side.

"I sure wish your mother would quit sending her spirit to visit me. She needs to come back here and sit her butt in that chair!"

With a shared chuckle, I sat on the edge of the bed and clasped her hand which, surprisingly, felt cool to the touch. Grandma's lucidity returned and, judging by the tiny sweat beads dotting her forehead, I knew her fever had vanished as fast as it had appeared.

"I love you, Grandma,"

"I love you too."

"You do know you have to get better, don't you? We promised one another that neither one of us would die until we met Jesus in

117

the clouds to—to—together." My voice broke as my mind dipped into the possibility this very well could be the time the infamous promise would be broken.

Her fingers squeezed mine. "I know." She cocked her head to one side. "I'll do my best to fulfill it." She cleared her throat. "I *promise.*" A sly smile curled her lips.

I cocked an eyebrow, as I bestowed my own playful grin. "I see."

Within seconds the lighthearted banter vanished as silent questions swirled before me; the sudden onset of unshed tears blurred my vision. *What if you can't, Grandma? What am I going to do without you in my life?*

A lump formed in the back of my throat, blocking further words. I warred against the urge to release the building pressure of my dammed-up emotions, but I didn't want to upset *Goose* with the deluge of tears I knew would flood the room if I let them flow.

The door pushed open and a young C.N.A. entered the room, her arms filled with soap, shampoo, lotion, clean towels, hospital gown, and linens for the bed. "Ready for your sponge bath, Hazel?"

Thankful for the interruption, I backhanded the moisture from each eye and stood. "I need some fresh air anyway, Grandma. Maybe some food too. Can I bring you anything?"

She shook her head. "I'm good."

I bent to kiss her cheek. "Okay. I'll be back before you miss me."

"Doubtful."

With a forced smile, I left.

With tears now streaking down both cheeks, I pressed the elevator button.

With heart-wrenching sobs filling the small empty space, I rode it to ground level.

***

Day ten came too early. It was time to return home to Idaho Falls, Idaho. We shared a last tight hug. "I promise I'll return if you need me, Goose."

"I'll be okay, Honey."

"I know."

Instead of letting go, her arms tightened around me and I squeezed her back just as tight.

Parting was *not* sweet sorrow. The chance we might not ever see or hug one another again in this world was all too real. And we both knew it.

While I was away, my grandma's health continued its ride on the mysterious roller coaster.

One day she seemed to be getting better.

The next?

Worse.

I phoned her room every single day to see how she was doing; I cherished the sound of her sweet voice as we'd converse back and forth.

December 7th, 1996 I got *the* early morning call that broke my heart: Goose's organs were failing, and they'd given her 24 hours to live.

My husband, our four children, and I threw suitcases in our white high-topped van and took off in a blinding blizzard. Boise was a five-hour drive; back then 55mph was the speed limit. We averaged between 35 and 45mph the entire trip as Idaho highways can be most treacherous in the winter. Respect for the conditions was crucial to living. Or at best arriving in one piece.

Eight hours had passed by the time we reached the hospital. The easy availability of Cellphones was non-existent at this time so, with trepidation Goose may have already left this world, I hurried to her room.

Thank you, God; she was still with us.

I had *not* missed my chance to say goodbye.

***

The next portion of this story I fashioned into a prologue for one of my romance novels *The Author and the Cover Model.* I was in the midst of writing the book when my grandma left this earth and I wanted to share my experience with others. It was written in third person and I have decided to keep it that way. Also, to leave the character names, descriptions, and the fate of KaLoni Kalamaiia's parents as fictionally written; a few things were changed for the sake of the novel.

And I'd like to share it with you now....

***

So, it was to end here.

She was going to lose the only person who had ever loved her, ever showed her any affection, here, in this medicinal cell-like cubicle.

"Don't leave me," KaLoni begged against her grandmother's feverish hand.

She stared at the elderly woman she loved with all her heart. Hair the color of the black sands of Hilo had only lately begun to whiten. Eyes the color of a stormy evening sky, so vibrant and aglow with life, lay closed in unnatural slumber. Her breathing was harsh, strangled. The nurses called it 'the death rattle.'

Gently returning the hand she held to her grandmother's side, KaLoni sank back in the bedside chair she had been occupying for hours. She sighed, searching the dimly lit room through swollen tear-stained eyes.

If only she could have taken Kupuna wahine home, surrounded her with the things she cherished. If only they could have celebrated this one last Christmas together. Perhaps then it would be easier to let her go?

No.

Nothing will make this easier.

KaLoni swiped the fresh tears from her face. Chest aching, stomach churning, she tilted her head skyward and stared at the ceiling. *Akua ma Lani (God in Sky Heaven) how can I just sit here and watch her die?*

Fear blended with her sorrow.

She wanted to run.

Hide.

Bury her mind in senseless denial.

But she couldn't.

Kupuna wahine needed her; she had to be brave.

She stood, grabbed three washcloths from off the counter, and went to the sink. Dousing them with cool water, wringing out the excess, she returned to the hospital bed to press two of the cool clothes into her grandmother's hot palms. Kupuna wahine always carried a wet washcloth when she felt under the weather and KaLoni knew she would appreciate this minuscule act of kindness.

Sitting on the edge of the bed, she took the remaining cloth, folded it in thirds, and laid it across her grandmother's forehead. With a light motion she used the cloth to smooth back the sweat-drenched curls lining the wrinkled brow. She bent over, kissing one precious cheek.

Her lips lingered.

How many more times will I be able to do this?

She straightened, swallowing against the unwelcome lump threatening to constrict her throat. Why did life have to end? Why so cruelly? Wasn't mankind made in God's image? Weren't we made to be eternal beings like Him? If so, no wonder she hated death—a human being's spirit was never meant to be ripped from its body.

Damn Eve.

Damn Adam.

With a trembling hand, she took up the cup setting on the tray-table, grasped the mouth swab, and dabbed the small pink sponge against the cup's lip. She lifted the oxygen mask from her grandmother's mouth, positioned it to rest beneath her chin, and placed the swab inside. With care, she rolled it about. How long had it been since Kupuna wahine had taken a real drink? Forty-eight hours? Although she had an IV drip keeping her hydrated, her mouth was parched from the one-hundred-percent oxygen she was receiving; blood lined her dry cracked lips. The nurses said the swabbing would help relieve the obvious discomfort.

Finished, she replaced the oxygen mask. "Rest now. I won't leave you." Reaching to the tray-table, she switched on the waltzing couples' music Christmas scene she had given her grandmother as an early Christmas gift, and turned the volume low.

The graceful movements of the tiny figurines waltzing magically across the mirrored dance floor took KaLoni's thoughts back to just last month. Her grandmother's reaction to the gift had been priceless....

"Oh, it's lovely, KaLoni. Why'd you do this? Christmas isn't for two more weeks."

"I wanted you to enjoy it now. I thought it might help lift your spirits and brighten up any old dark hospital room."

"You precious little thing."

"Those were the first words you said to me when you woke up from the coma. Do you remember?"

"No. I just remember staring into your beautiful face." Kupuna wahine took hold of KaLoni's hand.

"Thank you, Honey. I will treasure it as much as I do our time together." She reached toward the box. "Now, let's set this up so I can watch them dance."

With care, they removed each porcelain figure and freed them from the bubbled packing sheets. When they started to uncover the members of the orchestra, her grandmother squealed with delight.

"Look!" She held up the tiny piano player sitting before a baby grand piano. "It's your grandfather composing his gospel songs. Except," she tilted her head to one side, "he needs his glasses."

KaLoni took the figurine from her grandmother. "No need to fear when I'm here." She dug out a black pen from her fanny pack and set to making the man a replica of her grandfather, drawing small wire-rimmed glasses around miniature eyes, and darkening the orange hair to a splendid shade of auburn. Though she only had a few memories to cherish, she missed his presence in their lives...her grandmother had outlived him for over a decade.

Finished, KaLoni handed it back. "Kupuna kane."

Her grandmother's eyes misted. "Place him behind the verandah, Honey, and turn it on."

She did as she was told, then crawled onto the bed beside Kupuna wahine. She snuggled close, laying her head on the frail shoulder. Together, they listened to the waltz' of yesteryear, a precious time in her grandmother's life—a time with grandfather….

Let Me Call You Sweetheart played softly as KaLoni's focus returned to the here and now. It was Kupuna wahine's favorite. She watched the couples twirl for a moment before her eyes shifted to her grandmother's face. "What am I going to do without you? I'm only sixteen," she whispered aloud.

A shiver ran up her spine at the thought of living alone.

Her father had died when she was just young child and her mother had disappeared shortly thereafter.

The soon-to-come death of her grandmother would put her in a class of people she never imagined she would be a part of: an orphan.

The slow drumming of the oxygen, mixed with the irregular beating of the heart monitor, unnerved KaLoni.

She stood.

She paced.

She begged God for His divine intervention.

A moan from the bed had KaLoni back at her grandmother's side in seconds. "I'm right beside you."

Aged eyelids fluttered before opening. She spoke, but the mask muffled the near inaudible words she tried to form.

KaLoni lifted the mask once more.

"My—my prec…ious…precious…grandaughter."

"They told me you wouldn't wake up."

"They don't know everything." Her whispered words clearer, stronger.

"I love you, Kupuna wahine."

"I love you, too, Honey."

"Don't leave me."

A weak smile softened the pale face. "I will *never* leave you. I'm going to a place where I can *always* watch over you."

"I know. But it won't be the same. You won't be here to hold and encourage me. I don't think I can bear losing you—" KaLoni's voice crumpled.

Her grandmother's shaking hand rose to her face, vein-covered knuckles brushed her cheek. "Yes. you can. Look at yourself? How many people stay by their loved one's side, knowing death is near? You have an inner strength only *Akua* can give, and He gave it to you because you're special. *Always* remember that...*always*."

KaLoni nodded. She grasped a clean Styrofoam cup and filled it with fresh water from the plastic pitcher also occupying a spot on the tray-table. Placing the thin straw to her grandmother's lips, the water disappeared in several deep draws.

Kupuna wahine finished with a grateful smile. "Thank you for all you've done for me. You want to know something?"

"Yes."

"Raising you has been my finest accomplishment."

"Loving you has been mine." KaLoni grasped the frail hand caressing her cheek, and drew it to her lips. Her kiss lingered as she watched her grandmother's eyelids slowly close.

Electricity vibrated from the hand pressed against her lips. It intensified, traveling up KaLoni's arm until it showered over her head with an anointing force. For a moment her sorrow fled, and in its stead remained an uncanny peace.

The heart monitor flat-lined....

***

I wanted to share the above prologue with you, as the inner emotions KaLoni described to my readers were ones I felt at that time. However, there was a personal miracle that I did not include in the novel, a gold nugget so to speak, that I'd like to tell you about in this Christmas story.

An hour before *Goose* passed away, I was setting beside her, watching the Mrs. Clause doll I'd brought to her in the beginning. It set up high on a corner shelf to the right of the bed. She'd been turned on, so her arms opened and closed as her head nodded up and down with each action. The gold lantern nestled in her hands, lit the scene. Its light inhabited the doll's sweet face and, again with each movement, revealed two different emotions: a smiling Mrs.

Clause while down low and a more somber Mrs. Clause when the rays reflected beneath her chin.

While I was away, my grandma had told one of her nurses that each time the animated arms came together that was her *Charmie* giving her a hug. So, I was thinking of this when my gaze lowered to study the aged hand I held.

As I tried to memorize each vein, each knuckle, each finger, a light went out for a few seconds then came back on. I searched around the room, trying to figure out what bulb had flickered.

All was as it had been. There was no flickering light or a light that had gone out. Of course, if it had flickered, perhaps a cord had a short? Or a lightbulb was in the midst of burning out? My gaze lowered once more.

It happened again.

And again, several seconds later.

Each episode, I was unable to catch a glimpse of the source.

A few minutes passed by before the mysterious lack of light struck once more. This time my gaze shot up to Mrs. Clause. As her arms opened wide the lantern's light darkened; as they hugged back together, the light came on.

It was then the electricity KaLoni described began. It started in our clasped hands, traveled up the entire length of my arm, over my shoulder, and up my neck until the anointing shower flooded over the top of my head. And in that instant I knew what Goose was telling me: '*I'm not in that body racked with pain and unable to breathe…I'm up here, watching, floating, unlimited, happy, free of pain, free of mortality, ready to meet Jesus face to face.'*

Then a peace I'll probably never be able to explain inhabited my entire being. So much so, it flooded the room and I just knew any and all who entered would be able to feel it too.

Sadly, they couldn't. However, my claim such existed brought her son and his wife, her two daughters and their husbands, into the room to be with their mother when she left this world.

Christmas 1996…

The very date though once sad now brings me amazing joy.

I've since meditated on the miracles of my grandmother's entire earthly life and, as a preacher's wife, there were many. But, for me, the last were the greatest: the miracles we experienced the month we had with our *'lay-down comedian';* the miracle of a broken promise replaced with true and everlasting hope in a loving God, the miracle of peace she showed me minutes before stepping into Heaven.

My grandmother, Hazel Mildred Juanita Clark Silva, *our Goose*, taught me how to die without fear, without doubt of where I was heading. By existing between two worlds, having otherworldly visits, remaining faithful until the end, and using our Mrs. Claus lamp to reveal death is not our end, she proved the truth in several scriptures:

John 11:25 "Jesus said unto her, I am the resurrection, and the life: he that believeth in me, though he were dead, yet shall he live:"

129

"O, death, where is thy sting? O, grave, where is they victory?" *I Corinthians 15:55*

"Yeah though I walk through the valley of the *shadow of death*, I will fear no evil: for thou art with me; thy rod and thy staff they comfort me." *Psalms 23:4*

"Peace I leave with you, *my* peace I give unto you: not as the world giveth, give I unto you. Let not your heart be troubled, neither let it be afraid." *John 14:27*

I have felt that comfort—that uncanny peace Jesus left with us.

I have learned death is but a shadow…we live on in our new immortal bodies long after our old mortal bodies have decomposed.

So, if you've lost someone dear and they aren't around this Christmas, raise your head high. For you *will* see your loved one again, of this I am one hundred percent certain.

Hazel Mildred Juanita Clark Silva, my beautiful grandmother, preached the gospel most of her adult life. I'm certain I'd be in heavenly trouble if I didn't offer an altar call (so-to-speak) at the end of this story. So, I offer it below:

May we never forget the immense love that first Christmas brought us through the birth, life, death, and resurrection of Jesus Christ. **Give Him thanks**; He not only earned it, He deserves it and—

Give Him your whole heart for He truly is the friend that sticks closer than a brother. And He never counts your sin against you…His merciful grace covers up all that ugliness. If it didn't, then he died in vain and we believers know that that isn't the case.

He also promises to *never* leave nor forsake you, which means you are *never* alone. He is part of an amazing Heavenly Trio—Father, Son, and Holy Spirit, the other two loving you equally as much. What other god (or gods) in, on, above or below this world have ever offered more?

In Hazel's memory, I challenge you to open your bibles and get to know Jesus. Talk to Him on a daily basis…you don't have to pray form prayers. Just talk to Him like a friend. Let Him show you how much He loves you.

You'll *never* be sorry.

Merry *Christ*mas, dear readers!

ABOUT the AUTHOR: CHARM O'RYAN

Charm O'Ryan lives in Idaho Falls, Idaho with her husband of thirty-eight years. They have four grown children, five beautiful granddaughters; a handsome grandson here on earth, and another safe and happy in heaven.

Living on two and a half wooded acres, she enjoys her "slice of paradise". Summertime is her favorite season. She tends a koi and goldfish pond, outdoor flowers, and a four-hundred square foot vegetable garden. Nature provides the rest of her fun with owls, sparrow hawks, turtle doves, robins, magpies, hummingbirds, dwarf cottontail bunnies, squirrels, skunks, fox, raccoons, an occasional deer, and now feeds over twenty feral cats, who she tries desperately to catch and have them fixed. To date she has spayed and neutered eleven, put two down, and has her site set on five females and two toms in need of snipping! She encourages others to join her fight in controlling the homeless cat population. To date, she can pet thirteen of her twenty and believes that even feral cats (a.k.a. barn cats) can be loved and offer love in return. Charm, who has never had a cat her entire life, also loves dogs and has had a loyal canine companion or two beside her throughout her life.

An active member of The Blue Sage Writers of Idaho, Charm loves writing romance novels. She has five completed manuscripts, of which she self-published two: *The Table* **and** *The Author and The Cover Model.* She is currently working on a sixth and has grand ideas for several more. She loves creating memorable characters and placing them in difficult situations. She believes a strong plot is critical to romance writing—there has to be more than just love and sex.

One thing Charm guarantees her readers is that they will never forget her unique stories. She writes paranormal historical and contemporary; a great mix of time-travel, ghosts, angels, parodies about her genre, preachers' daughters and secret cops. She loves to laugh and cry and feels it's her job as a writer to take her readers on an emotional rollercoaster. But, never fear. The beauty of writing romance is that they ALWAYS end Happily Ever After.

Russian Tea Cakes

A Mangini/O'Ryan Family Christmas Tradition

Recipe provided by Charm (Mangini) O'Ryan

- 1 cup butter
- ½ cup powdered sugar (You will need at least 2 more cups of powdered sugar to use after cooking)
- 1 tsp vanilla
- 2 ¼ cups sifted flour
- ¼ tsp salt
- ¾ cup chopped walnuts

(Can triple all ingredients for larger amounts)

- Mix butter, powdered sugar, and vanilla together.
- Add flour and salt and stir until blended.
- Add walnuts and stir again. Roll into 1-inch balls and place on an ungreased cookie sheet.
- Bake at 400 degrees for about 10 to 12 minutes.

Check bottoms…tops will be a lighter brown. Put more powdered sugar in a large bowl. Remove teacakes from oven and as soon as you can handle them, roll them in the powdered sugar and place on cookie rack. Let them sit there for about 5 minutes and then roll in the powdered sugar again.

Charm's deviation from the recipe: Can add extra vanilla if you prefer. I always use two to three capfuls of the Vanilla bottle, not caring if it spills over into mix.

I've also taken my walnuts, placed them in a food processor, and ground them into a fine consistency. Then I add them to the teacakes. They are ground so well that if you have kids who turn up their noses at nuts being added, they'll never know the nutritious protein is inside! This is a tried and true experiment that I did with my own kids and grandchildren. Works like a Charm ... no pun intended. (Lol)

And last, but not least, you may roll your teacakes in the powdered sugar as much as you'd like. I usually repeat the process 3 or 4 times before placing them on a holiday platter and serving.

Warning: Russian Teacakes can be quite messy to eat, so be sure to eat over your hand or a bowl or a plate. Should some powdered sugar decorate your shirt, however, please know that the taste is well worth the dried mess.

Hope you enjoy our stories and...

"Merry Christmas!"

Borrowing Dickens' Ghosts

by Charm M. O'Ryan

One blustery December night, the bronzy midnight sky sparkling with the soft white seamless layers of snow clouds, I watched my favorite rendition of Charles Dickens's "A Christmas Carol," produced in 1970 and starring Albert Finney as the infamous Ebenezer Scrooge.

When it ended, I shut off the television and stared out the window, my thoughts tumbling as quick as the tiny intricate flakes of ice swirling to strike the misting glass. If I had the chance to borrow Dickens' ghosts, what would my personal journey be? Would I like what I saw? Or would I, like dear old cranky Ebenezer, see the personal flaws I possessed throughout my life? Would I see the world change as well?

Snuggled on the couch with a fuzzy throw, hot chocolate in hand, my attention shifted to the gas fireplace where bluish-orange flames danced against the fake logs. The face of the ghost of Christmas Past rose in the swirling smoke and, strangely, it resembled my great grandfather. Feeling total trust, I allowed the familiar, yet surreal, gaze to penetrate deep within the recesses of my mind and the specter's untimely thoughts, to meld with mine.

The past became my reality.

I saw my entire life of then, not yet now, flash before me in a second. A wee girl, sitting happily on mama's lap where I listened to stories of Christmas: the telling of the Christ child and how His appearance into life brought light unto the whole darkened world and offered great hope to the hopeless; I heard the tale of poor Rudolph and how he was shunned by all, and yet at the end became a hero. I saw myself falling asleep with excitement, my innocent dreams full of Santa's soon arrival to my house. Sweet kisses and warm hugs from my daddy, from precious grandparents, long since passed away, embraced me throughout those gentle years. I longed to stay in the memory of their love; to see them smiling and laughing and alive.

Then I was a teenager, having such fun as I discovered true and loyal friendships, felt the first stirrings of womanhood where I yearned for young and tender love, and went on to experience both the good and bad of its life-changing lessons. Pangs of regret filled my soul as I shattered the heart of my first boyfriend who I dated for three years; and crushed the heart of the second, whose unconditional love followed me my entire life, often making me ask the question, "What If?" *What if* I had said yes when he wanted to marry me as soon as we graduated high school? After a year and a half of dating, his desire to do so was reasonable. I saw his tears; felt his heartache. But I wanted to see the world—experience life. His feelings mattered not. At that time, it was all about me. I squeezed my eyes closed tight, attempting to clear the haunting vision of his intense pain and my overwhelming selfishness.

Next, I was a wife; then a mother by age twenty-one. It took me little over a year to learn marriage was *not* like the romance novels I'd read and, one day, would go onto write. My disappointment was grand, but I dealt with it. Reality was after all exactly that—reality. I went on to have four children. I saw their births and relived the euphoria of a new mother's joy. I smiled as I relived their first words, their first steps, their first hugs, their first kisses. My husband was a good provider but to do so he worked many long hours, missing so much that could never be replaced. Although he was my best friend, my soul grieved as the intense loneliness I'd felt all those years ago, returned to haunt me. I shook it off.

Appearing outside the house we'd raised our children in for eighteen years, my soul's warmth ebbed away. It stood silent, void of family, void of life. A *For Sale* sign anchored into the dirt, stood beneath the fifteen-foot birch tree. This house didn't deserve to be in such a state of isolation—the happiness and passion it'd given me, the protection I'd felt throughout the years, the creativity that flowed within its walls to my fingertips urging me to write five novels, demanded it be loved and taken care of. I pulled my sleeve down over my hand and wiped the steam from a corner of the window. Scenes from yesteryear lit the darkened room and my heart warmed with the immense love the walls once housed. Though at times bad things happened, as no life is perfect, within the safety of my old home I faced each obstacle, overcoming them with optimism, courage and faith. I just knew our family strength would survive anything that came our way.

The room darkened and great sadness flooded through me. I didn't want to leave, but the Ghost of Christmas Past took my mind elsewhere.

A split film screen stood before me and both my sons entered one side; my daughters, the other.

With joy, and worry, I watched my eldest girl marry and, with pride, my youngest graduate college. A smile curled the corners of my mouth. The arrivals of our first granddaughter and, later, first grandson, and the blessing their sweetness brought filled my soul with warmth. At that stage in our lives, my husband was able to stay home more and the role of grandma and papa brought fulfillment to our then twenty-six years of our marriage.

With intense dread, I watched my eldest son's horrific automobile accident and his struggle to regain his health to which he never truly did, constant pain holding him prisoner for years to come. Coinciding with the specter's clock, I stood helpless as I saw the youngest son get hooked on drugs and eventually arrested. As a mother, I felt both accomplishment and failure, the latter more pronounced, as I felt I had failed to protect my sons—failed to teach the baby the tremendous difference between right and wrong, slavery and freedom, life and death through the decisions we make in this life.

What a rollercoaster of flashbacks…flashbacks from one extreme to the other.

I wanted off the bipolar ride.

My body trembled. I stared at the Ghost. "I wish our bittersweet journey to end." Though the past held great joy, it also held great pain, great regret.

And I wished to view it no longer.

The subtle crackling of a fire floated to my ears. My vision cleared and I found myself back inside the living room of our newly remodeled house. Had I really gone anywhere? Or had my writer's imagination ran wild? I glanced at the antique Mission-style grandfather clock to my side. The brass hands pointed to eleven thirty-one. If I truly had journeyed from the present to the past, why had only four minutes elapsed since the movie ended?

A yawn escaped me. I had my answer. I had simply dozed off to sleep for a few sparse moments and dreamed. My eyelids heavy, I laid my head on the arm of the couch and, listening to the soft ticking of the key-wind clock, drifted off once more.

I was trudging through the snow when I saw her, my grandmother Hazel. She stood at the end of the driveway, waving me forward. No fear at all, I hurried to her side. She took hold of my hand and at her soft touch I knew the Ghost of Christmas Present had found me. With the tilting up of one side of her mouth and the wink of a brilliant blue eye, we rose in the air....

Flying beneath the stars, we passed by many stores and businesses, caught up in the busyness of the Christmas season. The words "Happy Holidays" echoed from the door-greeters of the hundreds we flew over; only two shouts of "Merry Christmas" rose amidst the bunch. Now over the residential section of town, I noticed only a handful of nativity scenes lit within the night. Sadly, I recognized the extreme difference *time* had taken in my life. Gone were the days of innocence, of small town America and the recognition of *the* God who blessed and protected her daily. The present held days of ignorance, pride in self, and the recognition that God's blessings and protection were no longer needed nor wanted. A tear escaped the corner of my eye, as I realized this hadn't just happened in my own small town. No. The entire country had fallen prey to the same idiotic lie the world concocted: we must *not* offend anyone. Unfortunately, Jesus' name did just exactly that to a handful of people. Thus, the double standard arose: we must not offend anyone *other than* Christians. Their rights could, and should, be abolished, as they had been deemed right wing extremists, troublemakers.

Shouldering the moisture from my cheek, I looked up at the unearthly woman holding my hand and wondered where my grandmother's gentle spirit was taking me. The mystery was soon solved as we landed outside my husband's office. Strange, I thought to myself, *why would the Ghost of Christmas Present bring me here?*

We went inside, levitating up and through the walls until we stood beside his desk. Bent over the computer, he was doing the weekly books, seeing how much money we'd made or lost, logging-in payroll for the employees hired at our restaurants, and paying the regular household bills. Worry drew harsh lines across his handsome face; deep concern furrowed his brow. It was as if he held the entire weight of the world upon his shoulders.

I wondered what was causing his stress and stared at the computer screen. I immediately saw we had lost money for the third month in a row. I glanced down at the opened checkbook resting on his desktop, and noticed the total was lower than it had been in years. The September 11, 2001 (911) attack on the World Trade Center and the war that followed, struck our country's finances hard. We were still recuperating from the massive losses when the housing market bubble burst seven years later. The current recession found its way to every town in America. And, like many others, our business suffered from its effects as contractors, realtors, home building supply companies and all those employed by such lost their jobs. People lost their homes as values turned upside down and banks panicked and began the steps of foreclosure. It was a real mess. Who had money to take their kids to a kid-centered restaurant with toys and video games?

No wonder my husband would come home in monstrous moods

No wonder he'd been distant and quiet at other times.

No wonder he'd asked me to be diligent in putting money aside, saying we might need it for a rainy day.

No wonder he'd told me not to go crazy buying Christmas gifts this year.

Guilt consumed me. I hadn't heeded his words, not knowing the true reason behind them. Of course, in my opinion, he shouldered some of the blame by not coming right out and telling me what was happening instead of dropping subtle hints. Honestly, I may not have believed him anyway, as our restaurants had always been successful, affording us a comfortable lifestyle. But now, seeing the evidence for myself, I had no choice but to concede to the truth.

All of a sudden, my husband looked old, tired, worn out both physically and mentally; his demeanor heartbreaking; his countenance distressing. I wanted to alleviate his suffering, hold him in my arms and tell him everything would be all right. I wanted to tell him that I'd do as he asked and be the best money saver he'd ever seen. However, I could do nothing but stand invisible at his side, powerless to offer comfort.

In the blink of an eye, we visited several homes: my eldest daughter's, where I heard her belief I loved her brothers and sister more than her; my best friend whose depression ran deeper than I had thought possible; another best buddy I had not visited in months, whose heart was failing at a rapid pace. I saw a couple of my fellow writers in our meeting room waiting for our meeting to start: they were sad over harsh critiques. They doubted their abilities as authors. I had once been the victim of such a critique and pledged to never put a fellow author through the heartache and discouragement I had felt. But had I done so unknowingly? Had I failed to keep my own promise and been too critical? My name came up and I felt two feet tall.

Before I knew what happened, The Ghost of Christmas Present whisked me back to my own house. We stood just inside the doorway to my daddy's room. He was crying as he spoke on the phone to my brother, explaining how he felt like a failure, how he tried to help but felt that that, too, was done clumsily and was unappreciated by all. He felt he couldn't do anything right...that everything he talked about from experience was challenged by a member of the family.

Stepping through the door to daddy's heart brought immense remorse. I don't care who you are or how well you think you can act when you take one of your parents into your home, it's much harder than you can ever imagine. They're old and set in their ways and think because they're the elder of the household they're the ones who should be in charge. It's a constant mental battle to play referee between your parent and your children and yes, even your husband. It wears a person down to say the least, so low you end up acting cold and indifferent, and say things you don't mean. But, they have become part of the family and have nowhere else to go. So what do you do? You have no choice but to grin and bear it and do your best.

And put up with your family's opinions and damning suggestions.

And live under a stress you pray your judges would never experience themselves.

Still, as I listened to daddy's sense of worthlessness, I knew if things did not change, he'd lose his will to live and I would be stuck with a thousand would-ah's, could-ah's, and should-ah's.

Gong…gong…gong…gong…gong…gong…gong…gong….

Through the haze of slumber, I listened as my clock struck the chords of twelve. Where was The Ghost of Christmas future? If the dong announced midnight it would be Christmas and too late to foresee more of what it is I am to change. Like Ebenezer, was I to be given the chance to set things right?

To be a better wife?

A better mother?

A better daughter?

A better friend?

Gong…gong…gong….

As the clock struck its twelfth and final *gong* my eyelids fluttered open and I found myself staring into a mirror. The truth dawned on me just as sure as the sun dawns on the horizon: the Ghost of Christmas Future was not an unseen specter or a figment of my sleep-laden imagination.

No, it was none other than—

ME!

I and I alone, held the power to summon change: one person, one action at a time, step-by-baby-step if that's what it took I could, and would, make the necessary alterations.

I didn't need some otherworldly spirit to show me I should run to my husband and tell him I love him and understand his concerns, that I will get a job to help out if that's what he wants.

I didn't need surreal guidance to assure my eldest daughter she is loved as much as the others. Or to tell an I.V. Heroin-addicted son that he will *never* leave my heart.

I didn't need an unearthly nudge to spend more time with my friends, to listen to *their* worlds for a change instead of being consumed with mine; nor to seek forgiveness from those writing buddies I didn't mean to offend…to make certain they know they are excellent writers!

I didn't need a spirit of any kind to know I can never change my past, only seek forgiveness from those I wronged; better my future by lessons learned from old mistakes.

I didn't need *The Ghost of Christmas' Yet To Come* to reveal the fact I should have more patience with daddy and his set-in-stone ways, to display as much love and appreciation in his direction as I can.

By borrowing Dicken's ghosts I found a valuable gold nugget: I, just one person lost in a sea of countless others, had the ability to revolutionize her world. Maybe not the world as a whole, not all at once anyway, but by being a better person inside and out, by standing up and remaining rooted in the truth of my ideals, using patience and love as my guide, maybe, just maybe those around me will be blessed...maybe nativity scenes will return to public property...maybe Jesus' name will become a blessing rather than a curse.

Who truly knows the difference one changed life can make?

Dicken's was an intelligent author to say the least. Using a fiction tale, he forced his readers to come face to face with their own shortcomings and mistakes, and then offered them the solution to fixing them: placing others above one's self, giving from the blessings one's received, and believing in our hearts that it's never too late for us to live a life we'll never bemoan.

I've now been married for thirty-eight years, surviving the occasional storms of marriage, and life in general, together. I have five beautiful grandchildren here on earth and one in heaven with my daddy. My mom and stepfather live with us now and I know

147

we'll all be happier for the change and will complain a whole lot less. I've realized that listening is *not* just waiting for one's turn to talk, and that love and forgiveness are what makes families stay together and friends become lifelong companions. Blessing those less fortunate, appreciating the little things alongside the big, have built my faith so much that I thank God every single day for the good, the bad, and the ugly that I experience. For I know that He takes the bad and makes it good; that He teaches valuable lessons through some of the darkest of times.

Perhaps Dicken's received a heavenly nudge to teach the world a thing or two?

I'd like to believe He did.

I do know one thing: God used Dickens to teach *me*. And I am eternally grateful.

"Merry <u>Christ</u>mas and—"

"God bless us all...everyone"

ABOUT the AUTHOR: CHARM O'RYAN

Charm O'Ryan lives in Idaho Falls, Idaho with her husband of thirty-eight years. They have four grown children, five beautiful granddaughters; a handsome grandson here on earth, and another safe and happy in heaven.

Living on two and a half wooded acres, she enjoys her "slice of paradise". Summertime is her favorite season. She tends a koi and goldfish pond, outdoor flowers, and a four-hundred square foot vegetable garden. Nature provides the rest of her fun with owls, sparrow hawks, turtle doves, robins, magpies, hummingbirds, dwarf cottontail bunnies, squirrels, skunks, fox, raccoons, an occasional deer, and now feeds over twenty feral cats, who she tries desperately to catch and have them fixed. To date she has spayed and neutered eleven, put two down, and has her site set on five females and two toms in need of snipping! She encourages others to join her fight in controlling the homeless cat population. To date, she can pet thirteen of her twenty and believes that even feral cats (a.k.a. barn cats) can be loved and offer love in return. Charm, who has never had a cat her entire life, also loves dogs and has had a loyal canine companion or two beside her throughout her life.

An active member of The Blue Sage Writers of Idaho, Charm loves writing romance novels. She has five completed manuscripts, of which she self-published two: *The Table,* and *The Author and The Cover Model.* She is currently working on a sixth and has grand ideas for several more. She loves creating memorable characters and placing them in difficult situations. She believes a strong plot is critical to romance writing—there has to be more than just love and sex.

One thing Charm guarantees her readers is that they will never forget her unique stories. She writes paranormal historical and contemporary; a great mix of time-travel, ghosts, angels, parodies about her genre, preachers' daughters and secret cops. She loves to laugh and cry and feels it's her job as a writer to take her readers on an emotional rollercoaster. But never fear. The beauty of writing romance is that they ALWAYS end Happily Ever After.

My Grandma Hazel's Christmas Divinity

Hazel Silva and Betty Mangini Christmas favorite recipe

Recipe offered by Charm (Mangini) O'Ryan

- ½ cup white corn syrup
- ½ cup water
- dash of salt
- 2 egg whites
- butter (for your hands)
- 1 and ½ cups chopped pecans

Place a medium or large saucepan on stove. Stir Sugar into Corn Syrup, water, and salt and turn on about medium high. Bring to a boil stirring constantly (do not boil on high…you don't want to burn it). Reduce heat to medium and continue stirring until either your candy thermometer reaches 240 degrees, or you test it old school: drop a spoon full of mixture into cold water and if it forms a medium-sized ball, it's ready.

As it nears readiness, beat the two egg whites until stiff in a separate pan. Once your sugar/syrup mixture is ready, pour 1/3 of it over stiff egg whites and beat constantly; add another third and keep beating; then add the rest until all is mixed well.

Cool at room temperature, without stirring, until lukewarm (by touch or about 110 degrees on candy thermometer). Place pan on a potholder to keep it from slipping and, again, beat the entire mixture until it holds its shape. At this point you may use an electric beater if your arm feels like it's about to fall off.

Butter both hands and kneed the cooling mixture until firm…be sure to keep your hands well-oiled so reapply butter as often as needed. Shape into two 1 and ½ inch rolls. Roll in the chopped pecans. Press nuts firmly into candy. Wrap in waxed paper and chill. Once candy roll is chilled, slice into ½ inch thick pieces.

Scrumptious!

And since you definitely got your exercise for the day with all that stirring, count your first piece of Divinity as calorie free. After all, it is Christmas and the time of year to believe in miracles! (Lol)

Christmas English Toffee Squares

Another O'Ryan favorite Christmas recipe
Recipe offered by Charm O'Ryan

- 1 cup (2 sticks) butter
- 1 cup sugar
- 2 cups sifted All-Purpose flour
- 1 egg yoke
- 1 egg white lightly beaten
- 1 tsp vanilla extract
- 2 cups finally chopped walnuts or pecans (sliced almonds are good, too)
- Coconut (if desired)
- Cinnamon (if desired)

Preheat oven to 350 F

Melt butter in a large saucepan. Add sugar, flour, egg yolk and vanilla. Mix well. Spread evenly in a 9 x 12 inch baking-pan. Press into pan. Spread lightly beaten egg white across the top of mixture and sprinkle evenly with chopped nuts.

Bake 20 minutes or until lightly browned. Remove from oven and let set in pan for 3 to 4 minutes. Cut into squares while still in pan. Cool thoroughly before removing. Recipe makes about 2 dozen squares.

My tweaking of recipe: This recipe can be doubled and put in larger 10 x 18 inch pan. Since my family loves coconut and cinnamon *before cooking* I sprinkle cinnamon, (as much or as little as you'd like) on top of the egg white after it is spread across the top. Then I add nuts and then the coconut, again, as much or as little as you'd like. I lightly press it all into the dough. Sometimes top cracks when you cut into squares, but the crumbs are mighty good too.

Enjoy!

A Visit From a Reindeer

by R. Peterson

I was getting much too old you see

In Santa Clause and reindeer
that come on Christmas Eve.

Better late than never.
I decided to find out
If Santa brought the presents
And coal for those who pout.

When the household went to sleep
I hid behind the tree
And prepared myself to wonder
At what I wouldn't see.

Beyond the stroke of midnight.
Beyond the hour of one.
A rustle in the chimney
Smoke and soot did come

I tried to wink my eyes awake
I roughly shook my head.
I even thought of waking up
My sleepy wife in bed.

I shouted out this cannot be
Santa isn't real
Then to my wonder and surprise
I saw hoof instead of heel.

Was no jolly-man dressed like an elf,
Who brushed the ashes off.
But a two-leg standing reindeer,
With red bag made out of cloth.

With snouty nose and antlered head
And fur-lined coat of red.
My thumping heart reminded me
I should have stayed in bed.

The creature cast his eyes about
He looked around the tree
Behind a wrapped up "walk and talk"
He finally spotted me.

He pointed to a plate of cookies there
Placed on the kitchen table.
They look good, don't get me wrong
I'd eat them was I able.

Santa loves the sweets and things
Left out for him to eat.
But he's sleeping in the sleigh right now.
Too sick to have a treat.

They say a cold is going round.
They say the flu is near.

But all we reindeer catch is wind.
No illness do we fear.

        I'm filling in for him you see
        My name is Nutter deer.
        Rudolph retired long ago.
        And grew fat drinking beer.

Prancer lives in Omaha
Dixon moved out west.
Comet married Cupid
And old age took the rest.

        The deer that pull this Christmas sleigh
        Don't sprinkle magic dust.
We download app on iPhone six
Technology we trust.

        We navigate by Google Earth.
        Skimming over drifts.
        We take MasterCard and Visa
        And no one wraps your gifts.

So eat those cookies there yourself
And drink that milk down too.
Santa would have loved them
If he didn't have the flu.

        I hunger for a salad
        So open fridge door wide.
        Do it now—I'm famished.
        I want to look inside.

For carrots, radish, celery
… and other things you hide.
No dressing on the lettuce
Just vegetables at side.

Don't pour me water in a glass
I drink from bowl you see.
Thirsty from the visits
We make on Christmas Eve.

And when he finished chomping
Grazing like a lamb.
He buttered me a slice of toast
And covered it with jam.

And now you've caught me eating, dear.
Alas his sleigh is gone.
And though my diet's broken
I've really done no wrong.

See the new coat under tree
That Santa brought for you
Delivered by a reindeer
Cause Santa has the flu.

Yes dear, I'll return to bed.
And wipe this jam from face.
And promise you that all I said
No lies will bring disgrace.

Will anyone accept the truth?
Will anyone believe?
In a reindeer name of Nutter.
That came on Christmas Eve.

158

The Cornflake Box
by R. Peterson

Johnny Miller was in a hurry so he dared a shortcut through Mr. McKinsey's Apple Orchard. The first snowflakes of 1952, drifting from the gray sky, resembled the Nutcracker Ballet from his second-grade Christmas program. The holiday performance took the place of all three afternoon classes. These dancers didn't scowl and fidget. They floated to the joy of winter dressed in shimmering frozen gowns.

A low growl made him slip and almost fall on the snow-covered ground. Butch rushed from the fence that separated the neighbor's property from theirs. The Pit-bull lab mix, snapped his jaws together in a vicious display of authority as it reached the end of a twenty-foot chain.

"Not today Butch!" Johnny laughed. "Mama had to put a big patch over the seat of those other pants you tore." The dog whined and began to wag its tail. "I'll see if I can sneak you out something from the kitchen later," Johnny whispered. He felt bad. The poor dog was fed only every third day. It was Mr. McKinsey's way of keeping the starving canine from going soft. Johnny vaulted the board fence… and was home.

Mary Miller stood at the sink washing dishes when Johnny banged open the kitchen door. "Go back and wipe off your feet; I just mopped," his mother scolded. Johnny slipped off his shoes on the entryway rug instead and ran into the living room. The tiny Christmas tree they decorated the night before, stood blocking the window in radiant glory. Red and blue glass balls shimmered against green pine needles draped with sparkling icicles. Strings of multi-colored twinkling lights would be plugged in after dinner.

The brilliant ornaments reminded Johnny of happier years. Grandfather and Grandmother had been alive then. These same decorations had covered their holiday trees, before the sickness that went around and struck everyone with deadly coughing. Somehow this Christmas seemed different, more anxious than any he could remember.

Johnny's heart sank when he noticed there still wasn't a single present under the tree. "When are we going to put out our gifts mother?" Johnny dragged one toe on the cold floor, through a hole in his stocking, as he skated back into the kitchen. "Jeff Jones' family has twenty-three wrapped presents under their tree. We counted them before we walked to school."

"Jeff's father has a good job working in the bank and they didn't have a Ford with a starter go out just two weeks ago." A soapy dish slipped from Mary's hand and crashed to the floor. A tear rolled down her cheek before she turned and dried her face with a dishtowel. "Grab me the broom and dustpan," she told her son.

Mary was smiling when Johnny returned. "Christmas Eve isn't until tomorrow," his mother said. "Your father should be home any time. I hope Mr. Manton was able to give his employees a bonus this year. If he did, maybe we can all go downtown after supper and buy a few things." Mary stared out the window as she rinsed the last dish. The snow was falling heavier now and a strong wind came from the North. John was late.

"Yippee!" Johnny danced around the kitchen until Mary set him to work peeling potatoes while she thumbed through Melania's old wooden recipe box. Mary's anxious brown eyes searched through the almost bare cupboards. A small package of sugar from her mother's house sparkled like angel dust as she poured it and what flour she had into a bowl.

Minutes later, the sound of roaring wind made Johnny and his mother both look. John Miller pushed open the kitchen door stomping heavy clumps of snow from his ragged work boots. A blast of cold air shoved past him settling everywhere inside the three rooms. Mary had just put a pan of sugar cookies in to bake. She rushed to make sure her husband's clomping didn't dislodge the broom handle wedged to keep the oven door closed.

Mary didn't want to look up. Somehow the way her husband stood on the tiny square rug without moving said more than words.

"Management told everyone the new factory they purchased in Butte cost a lot more to put into operation than they figured." John's thin voice broke. "There's no cash bonus this year." John placed a frozen chicken next to the sink. "Merry Christmas from Mr. Manton."

"I'll get this thawing," Mary said not looking at her husband. "It will make a nice Christmas dinner."

"We're still going shopping after dinner aren't we mom?" Johnny was tugging on his mother's apron.

"I'm sorry," his mother said as she bit her lip. "We'll still have us a wonderful Christmas even without gifts this year!"

Johnny burst into tears. "All my friends have presents to open even Tammy Haskel and she lives with her spider aunt and her brother's black widow."

Mary smiled in spite of her troubles. "That's spinster dear," She called after him as he ran into the living room. "It means she's never been married."

"I don't care," Johnny sobbed from under the tree.

Mary stared at her husband's back as he shivered next to a cracked window staring into the snow flurries.

"I know a way we can make almost ten dollars cash tonight," John turned. "Most of the stores in Cloverdale will stay open till five tomorrow on Christmas Eve. It will be one heck of a rough night but it can be done," he said.

"Ten dollars!" Mary's mouth gaped open. "How?"

"Ben Hayes delivers newspapers for The Vanishing River Tribune. He does the rural route that goes over Motha Pass one hundred and forty deliveries at seven cents per paper paid on completion. It takes him about six hours… us maybe eight. His Dodge station wagon broke an axel. He's looking for someone to take over his job just for tonight. The bundles have to be picked up downtown at two AM. So far, he hasn't had any takers. No-one wants to go out driving at night on these treacherous roads."

"But the tires on our car are almost bald," Mary cried.

"I have a tank full of gas and that set of rusty chains in the trunk your father gave me," John said. "Someone will need to ride with me, fold the papers and put them in the holders next to the mailboxes."

"I could ask Mrs. McKinsey next door to watch Johnny tonight," Mary was thinking. "She's grumpy and hard to get along with but I'll bet she could use a dollar and a half. Johnny would be asleep while she was here anyway."

John and his wife met in the center of the room and gave each other big hugs. "We will have us a Merry Christmas after all!" Mary laughed. "I better get started with those chains," John said.

Laughter came from the kitchen; Johnny didn't know what was so funny. This was going to be the worst Christmas of his life. The smell of fresh baked sweets drifted through the house moments before he heard his mother calling. "Johnny you better come eat one while they're hot!"

"I'm not hungry," Johnny wailed. He covered his ears with both hands.

164

Mary opened the refrigerator. There was much inside but there was enough milk for one glass. She poured it into a chipped cup next to the cookies. She didn't know about a lot of things but she did know her son. Johnny wouldn't sulk for long.

Mary was humming one of her mother Melania's favorite songs and rinsing the pan in the sink when she got an intuitive tug from her long dead mother. Why not, she told herself as she pulled a wooden crate filled with Melania's folded cardboard boxes, used wrapping paper and ribbons from a top shelf. Sugar from the cookies was still stuck to her fingers and spread to the gold foil. She didn't brush it off; it sparkled like glitter. Johnny would feel better about being left alone with Mrs. McKinsey if he had something to dream about.

Mary came into the room and squatted beside her son. Johnny kept his face buried in the empty white cloth under the tree. It wasn't until the swoosh of paper being pushed under the boughs crackled that he dared to peek. A ten inch long, gold foil covered box tied with a bright red ribbon lay against the tree stand. Johnny held his breath as he rose to his knees. A blue and green tag, he recognized from last year, was taped on one edge. *Merry Christmas Johnny* was printed on top.

"I love you mom," Johnny said as they walked into the kitchen. He wouldn't let go of the wrapped box and ate two cookies and drank the milk with one hand. They sang *Frosty the Snowman* together and talked about playing outside in the snow the next day.

-------*------

Johnny woke warm in the fold-down bed in the living room. He slept with three blankets while his mom and dad slept with one. They were talking to Mrs. McKinsey in the kitchen. Johnny looked at grandma Descombey's old clock on the table next to the sofa. 1:30 am. He thought at first he'd been dreaming, until he sat up on the mattress and stared at the brightly lit tree glowing with every color. There beneath the green branches was the box, wrapped with gold foil and tied with a red ribbon. He didn't have to look at the tag to know his name was on it. He smiled as he pulled the heavy blankets over his head and drifted off to sleep.

-------*-------

A cold wind swept into the room and Johnny woke to loud voices. Mrs. McKinsey from next door was talking and she sounded angry. "Why wasn't I told about this sooner? I could have been home in my own bed instead of trying to endure this filthy house these people keep." Two police officers, one old and one young stood in the open doorway as Johnny entered the room pulling on a frayed wool sweater.

"Is this the boy?" The older one pointed a gloved finger at Johnny. Mrs. McKinsey nodded then looked away. The younger officer looked at the other, then shrugged his shoulders. "I'm sorry to tell you this son, but your parents were in a bad accident with a semi-truck. That fool driver was hauling a loud of fuel oil when he went out of control up on Motha Pass last night."

Johnny looked at the two officers; both their faces were white. "Is my mom and dad... are they in the hospital?"

"There was a terrible fire," the older policeman stammered. "I'm afraid your folks was both pronounced dead at the scene."

Johnny stared from one face to the other, no one in the room would look at him. He sat at the table and pushed crumbs from the empty cookie plate into tiny piles. "We're going to make a snowman, me and mom." He smiled but couldn't catch an eye. "When dad comes outside to shovel the sidewalk were going to hit him with snowballs." Johnny tried to laugh, anything to break the silence but his voice sounded strange even to his own ears.

"Can you watch the boy until someone from Social Services can get here?" The older officer was asking Mrs. McKinsey.

"I'm not the boy's mother, thank the Good Lord," Mrs. McKinsey grumbled. "I don't know how I'm going to be paid for my babysitting now!" She glared around the room then at both policemen.

"I'll make sure you're compensated for your time," the younger cop promised.

"Looks like I don't have a choice," Mrs. McKinsey said. A cold wind howled outside as she slammed the door behind the officers.

Johnny watched as his neighbor dumped the crate filled with wrapping paper on the floor then pulled the thawing chicken from the sink. She emptied the refrigerator and cabinets stuffing everything into the large wooden box. "I'll be damned if I'm leaving here empty handed," she said. Mrs. McKinsey carried the box into the living room and laughed as she stared at the tiny pine. "What are you people, a bunch of hobos?" She cursed as she plucked bulbs from the tree and carelessly tossed them into the crate.

The golden present under the branches next to the tree stand caught her eye just as she turned. Mrs. McKinsey snatched it up the same time Johnny cried "That's mine!"

"Shut your mouth before I slap you," she promised.

The neighbor turned the box over in her hands a scowl on her face. She snickered as a torn place on the bottom showed the corn flake box inside. "Garbage! Like everything else you got in here!" She flung the present to the floor and filled the crate the rest of the way with items from the room.

"I'm taking this stuff to my house. If anybody asks it was owed to me... do you understand?" Johnny was silent, speechless until she kicked him.

"Yes, mam."

"Them cops show up again, you tell them I want my damn money!"

"I will," Johnny said.

Mrs. McKinsey walked out carrying the heavy box and kicked the door closed behind her.

The silence was strange without the ticking of grandmother Descombey's clock. Johnny picked the gift his mother had wrapped from the floor and looked at it from every angle. The corners of the foil paper were tucked neatly at each side and the red ribbon tied with loving care. He could sense his mother's presence as he removed the bow. The tape holding the sides took a long time to peel away without damaging the wrapping paper but Johnny did so. Finally the Kellogg's Corn Flake box lay unwrapped in his trembling hands.

He said the kind of prayer only an eight year old boy can say, in a humble quiet voice as he opened his gift. It was as he expected, empty inside.

Johnny gulped and closed his eyes. Perhaps he was wrong… no not completely empty. He could smell his mother's cookies baking. That warm wonderful fragrance, that meant he was in a loving home, lingered on the wrapping paper along with something mysterious and magical. A rustling sound spread from the Earth across the galaxy then throughout the universe as the fabric of time shifted. The wind ceased to howl and he listened to the sound of a car stopping outside. A dog's excited barking. It must be the people the police said would come for him. His tears were late in arriving, but now they rolled down his face in waves.

His mother's voice called from the kitchen. "Johnny you better come eat one while they're hot!"

Johnny held his breath sure it was imagination, until she called again. He slowly staggered into the kitchen with unbelieving eyes. His mother was taking a hot pan filled with sugar cookies from the oven. She yelped as the broom handle holding the door fell and the heavy metal banged her knee. "Your dad isn't getting any of these until he fixes that," she laughed.

The kitchen door pushed open and John Miller stomped heavy clumps of snow from his ragged work boots. "I got it!" he yelled. "A hundred dollars for a Christmas bonus!" He held the five twenty-dollar bills in the air as his wife squealed with delight. Johnny's father looked at his son. "I've got something for you too." He turned as Butch padded in behind him shaking snow off his fur and wagging his tail. "Mr. McKinsey said he was tired of feeding his dog and was taking him to the pound to be put to sleep. I told the old coot I didn't think that was such a good idea."

Johnny's mom made a fuss about cleaning the snow off her kitchen floor while he and his father played with Butch by the tree. "We better hurry if we want to get all our shopping in before the stores close." Mary said when she finished. She pointed to the unwrapped corn flake box under the tree. "I'm sorry about the trick," she told Johnny. "We all need things to believe in, to keep hope alive."

"That's okay mom," Johnny said. He looked around the room. True joy surged through his soul. He laughed as the Christmas Spirit settled, like a warm blanket, on his precious family. "Sometimes the greatest gifts are things you don't get."

THE END

ABOUT the AUTHOR: RANDALL R. PETERSON

Randall Peterson normally writes horror or mystifying fiction, so we are happy to include a Christmas story, totally out of his usual genre, by this talented author.

Randall writes the "Cloverdale: Tales of Terror" series available on Amazon, and has a blog - randallrpeterson.blogspot.com

CORNFLAKE BARS – MAKES ABOUT 16

INGREDIENTS

- 3 cups corn flakes, crushed
- 1 cup crunchy peanut butter
- ½ cup sugar
- ½ cup white corn syrup

INSTRUCTIONS

- Heat peanut butter, sugar and corn syrup over low heat to melt
- Stir in cereal.
- Pat into an 8x8 lightly greased pan. (I line my pan with foil and then lightly spray it. When it is time to cut them, the foil lifts right out.).
- Melt chocolate chips over low heat or in the microwave and spread over top.
- Cool until firm, cut into bars and enjoy!.

The Game

by Richard Earl Rice

Dian bent down, picked up a few sticks of kindling, thrust them into the flames, and slid the metal lid back over the hole. She stood for a moment in the stove's warmth, feeling heat through her thin, faded, cotton dress. Welcome heat, but not enough to fully chase away the constant chill she'd endured since winter had hit them. She rotated to warm her back and swept her gaze over the crude surroundings inside the tiny cabin.

A tattered calendar hung over her cot on the far wall. She had religiously crossed off every passing day since The Burning. Tomorrow would be their first Christmas as survivors of a catastrophe she still didn't fully understand. She choked back a sob, afraid she'd wake the kids.

She ran a hand through her hair, hanging in spindly drifts, dirty beyond belief. She could hardly remember what it had been like to take a hot shower and wash her hair. In the former time, her long blonde tresses had been her pride and joy. Mike's too. She longed for those days, a happier time, now gone forever.

She walked across the dirt floor to the bunks and checked the children's covers. She snugged grimy blankets around the tiny forms, trying not to disturb their naps. When they were sleeping, their minds were not on the cold. Or the hunger.

173

Sean's eyes popped open. "When's Daddy going to be back?"

She shook her head, tears forming in her eyes. "I don't know, honey," she said, stroking his forehead. It took a huge effort to mask her own fears. Since the solar wind had swept over the planet, humanity had descended into chaos. Mike thought things were a little better now, since nearly everyone out there had died during the ensuing year. But there were still a few surviving on remnants of the old world who would kill you for a warm coat.

She was surprised she, Mike, and the kids were not dead too. Maybe it would be better if they were. But this old cabin, on the flanks of the Yellowstone plateau, had been their salvation. Out of the way, far from roads, the hands of some long-dead miner had left an antique refuge. On that last family backpack trip, they'd chosen to sleep in this place. It turned out to be a lifesaving choice, as the heavy logs shielded them that night from waves of ionizing radiation. Afterwards, they just stayed, knowing a return to the city meant almost sure death from the starving masses.

Mike had been gone for three days now. He'd been an opportunist over the past year, keeping his family alive in a hostile world. He ventured out often, making forays into abandoned cabins, or stores. He came back with food, clothes, once even a .22 rifle and a box of ammunition. The rifle had played a big role in their survival. Small game made decent table fare if you were starving. And once, Mike had to kill a desperate man who'd broken into their cabin, intent on stealing everything they had.

174

Just when she expected she'd be spending another night alone, worrying about Mike, she heard sounds outside the door. Wary as always, she grabbed a kitchen knife and peered out a frosty window into the twilight. Mike was there on the porch, unbuckling his snowshoes. The door creaked open, and he stepped inside, dropping his pack on the floor. He set the rifle against the wall, then swept her into his arms. His face was gaunt and gritty, but she didn't care. He was home.

She looked into his eyes. "How was it?" she asked.

"Went all the way to Ashton. Pickings were slim, but I did pretty good." He lifted the pack and dropped it on the table. Reaching inside he pulled out a can of spam and two potatoes. Also a few other cans - vegetables, fruit and soup. Enough for a few meager meals, she thought, heart wrenching. She wished he'd found more.

Next he extracted a pair of jeans and a ratty sweatshirt. "These should fit you," he said touching her worn dress. He'd also scavenged a pair of shoes for Sean and a tiny coat for Misty. The sack contained one last item - a small package, wrapped in brown paper, tied with string.

She hefted the spam and potatoes. "Well, at least we'll eat tonight." She put a skillet on the stove and spooned in some lard. She looked at the little package. "What's this?"

"A Christmas present," he said, taking a seat at the table. "Something for all of us."

She didn't know what to say. They were on the brink of starving and freezing and he brings back something frivolous. She hid her disappointment and began slicing the potatoes, dropping them into the bubbling grease. She slid the spam out of the tin and cut slices as thin as possible, so the meal would seem larger than it really was. She slid the meat in with the potatoes and stirred the mixture with a spatula.

The kids came to the table wrapped in blankets and the four of them picked up forks. "Eat slowly, children," she said, dishing up the meal. "Make the food last as long as you can." They ate in silence, finally wiping the last remnants of grease from their plates. Afterwards, she cleaned up, rejoined the others at the table, and lit a candle. They all stared at the little string-wrapped package.

"Anyone want to open our Christmas present?" Mike asked.

Sean lifted the box, held it by his ear, and shook it. "I will."

The boy carefully undid the string and unwrapped the paper, saving everything in case the items might come in handy later. He picked up a small box, adorned with pictures of black tiles covered with white spots. "What are these?" the boy asked, shaking it again.

"It's a game," Mike said with a hint of a smile.

"A game?" Sean asked, lifting the box. "How do you plug it in?"

Misty reached out and touched the box. "Can't plug it in, Sean. We got no 'lectricity."

"Don't need electricity," Mike said. He explained the rules of dominoes and they began to play. First Mike and Sean against Dian and Misty. Then they swapped partners and played some more. Finally, it was kids against the adults. Snapping the tiles down on the table, they began to laugh as the excitement got to them.

A strange, pleasant feeling came over Dian, listening to her family at play. They had seldom smiled over the past year, and never laughed. If this game of dominoes could replace hopelessness with joy, she knew at that moment they could survive this holocaust.

She and Mike exchanged glances. His eyes were bright. She could tell he felt a measure of hope too.

"Merry Christmas, everyone," she said.

ABOUT the AUTHOR: RICHARD EARL RICE

Richard brings a unique blend of work experience and life interests to his writing career. Besides his engineering background, he holds a Commercial Pilot's license, operates his own aircraft, serves as Director for an oil company, and manages a substantial portfolio of commercial and residential real estate.

Richard's main writing interest is Speculative Fiction, where he extrapolates current events and difficulties from our present society into worlds filled with unique problems for his characters to deal with. He tries to make his projections plausible, ones that will perhaps serve as warnings to his readers that we are living in an exponentially unstable time and significant changes can be expected that may not be good for our descendants.

He has produced five novels and a number of short stories. Richard can be found living on the Snake River in Southeastern Idaho near Yellowstone Park and Jackson Hole, or at his winter getaway in Southern Utah, near Zion Park.

Find out more about Richard and how to obtain his books on his website at www.richardearlrice.com or go to Amazon.com and search under books for Richard Earl Rice.

A Different Kind of White Christmas

by Richard Earl Rice

Years before I resettled in Idaho, I spent my youth in Southern California, land of fruits and nuts. Most of my growing up days, blessed with mild winters, my friends and I would hike into the foothills on the weekends, or play endless games of baseball or football in the afternoon before our moms called us in for supper.

I never understood what Bing Crosby meant when he dreamt so soothingly of a White Christmas, but Mom and Dad, who were transplanted from Michigan, apparently did, as they often sang along with Bing, sometimes a little teary eyed. But in San Bernardino, Christmas was always green, or brown, with sometimes a spot of rain. White Christmases only visited us in song lyrics and figments of our imaginations.

But there was that one year I'll never forget. I was about twelve. On a Friday morning, December 23, I awoke to the ear-splitting shrieks of my younger sister, running amok through the house, barefoot in her nightgown. "Snow, snow, snow," was all she could say, racing from window to window. Somehow the weather patterns had worked up a "perfect storm" and our little town was buried in about six inches of fresh, white, cold, wonderful snow, and more was falling as we stared in wonder out the frosty windows.

In Idaho, as I learned much later, a six-inch snowfall was greeted with a resigned shrug before getting on with your day—to work, to school or simply to pick up a snow shovel and have at it. But on that day in California, our panicked city fathers declared a major emergency, shutting down the entire town. Schools, offices, banks, store—all closed. Did you hear that? Schools were closed according to the radio broadcast on the emergency channel, set up by the government to warn us of Russian nuclear attacks.

Every kid I knew, thus liberated, never considered breakfast that day. All thoughts of Christmas, coming two days hence, were buried by that miraculous snowpack. Out into the white stuff we sped, typically clad in levis, ragged jackets, thin cotton gloves, and black Keds tennis shoes. On the second fairway of the nearby golf course, we built snow forts and stocked up with snowballs, then made war. We carved out snow angels. We slid down hills seated on shovels, the only snow transportation available, since none of us

California kids had sleds, skis or snowshoes. We played Fox and Geese and ran around with our heads back, mouths open, trying to catch that one particular snowflake we picked out of the swarm falling to earth. Snowmen could be spotted on nearly every front lawn. It was non-stop action.

All red-faced, soaking wet and cold, we took occasional breaks to warm up, have a quick bite and put on dry clothes before racing out to resume the adventure. But these breaks only lasted for minutes. The snow was calling.

It seemed as if that day and the next passed in a flash. The impending Christmas was all but forgotten and every kid in town put all his energy into the miracle of snow. By Friday afternoon, the snow stopped falling and the wise men in charge of our city declared the disaster over. At dawn on Saturday, Christmas Eve day, the snow was still there, waiting for us to rise and suit up again. And we did with as much enthusiasm as the day before.

Later that day, as the clouds blew away, carrying the snow off to Utah and maybe Idaho, we witnessed an awesome Christmas eve sunset, bright clouds laced with a dozen shades of red. As darkness drew upon our city, thousands of wet, cold, and thoroughly exhausted kids dragged their aching bodies back to their homes to warm up, eat, fall into bed and presumably dream of sugar plums.

Our usual warm and sunny California weather returned to us on Christmas morning. As we all engaged in our unique family rites of Christmas, the sun did its work, eating the beautiful white snow.

By the end of that day, the white stuff was nearly gone, except in shady spots and a few lumps on the golf course, the dying remnants of our snow forts. By the next day, only traces of the snow remained.

But what a time we had, if only for a couple of days. I have to say, the Great Snow Adventure is still vivid in my mind, decades later. I have no idea what was waiting for me under the tree that year, which of our relatives came to visit, or what we ate for Christmas dinner. But the snow memories linger yet. They will never leave me. It had to have been the greatest Christmas ever.

ABOUT the AUTHOR: RICHARD EARL RICE

Richard brings a unique blend of work experience and life interests to his writing career. Besides his engineering background, he holds a Commercial Pilot's license, operates his own aircraft, serves as Director for an oil company, and manages a substantial portfolio of commercial and residential real estate.

Richard's main writing interest is Speculative Fiction, where he extrapolates current events and difficulties from our present society into worlds filled with unique problems for his characters to deal with. He tries to make his projections plausible, ones that will perhaps serve as warnings to his readers that we are living in an exponentially unstable time and significant changes can be expected that may not be good for our descendants.

182

He has produced five novels and numerous short stories. Richard can be found living on the Snake River in Southeastern Idaho near Yellowstone Park and Jackson Hole, or at his winter getaway in Southern Utah, near Zion Park.

Find out more about Richard and how to obtain his books on his website at www.richardearlrice.com or go to Amazon.com and search under books for Richard Earl Rice.

RASPBERRY BRIE APPETIZER

INGREDIENTS
- Puff pastry sheet – thawed

- 8 oz raspberry jam
- 1 egg - beaten

INSTRUCTIONS
- Place Brie cheese in freezer for 30 minutes

- Slice partially frozen Brie cheese into 2 equal discs

- Place one disc in center of puff pastry sheet

- Spread raspberry jam over Brie disc

- Place second Brie disc on top

- Fold puff pastry over Brie-jam discs using beaten egg as glue

- Place upside down and bake on greased pan at 425F for 25 minutes.

Serve with your favorite cracker. Enjoy!

Turning Point

by Sherry Roseberry

Agnes clutched her threadbare coat tighter to her chest in a vain attempt to block out the biting chill. Frowning, she stood on the street corner and watched the traffic whiz by. A group of teenagers, joy riding in a blue van, swerved, splashing icy slush onto her dirty gray trousers. The van sped on, and she heard the faint strains of laughter. Her ever-present scowl deepened.

"And a very Merry Christmas to you, too," she spat out as she watched the receding taillights.

Heaving a tired sigh, the old lady stepped down from the curb. Pain shot up from her hips to center in her back. Her janitorial job left her with sore muscles every night, and tonight proved no different. The steady ache across the top of her shoulder blades heightened, and she longed for her soothing ointment, a heating pad, and bed.

She stuffed her bare hand deep inside the tattered pocket of her pants and felt the small package. Her boss had suggested that she leave early and then had given her the present, wishing her a Merry Christmas. She had only grunted a curt reply as she shuffled to the coatroom. Ordinarily, she would've insisted on finishing her work, Christmas Eve or no Christmas Eve, but she tired so easily these days.

Christmas! Who needs it? All it did was make people go around with silly smirks on their faces. Besides, it caused parents to shower presents on ungrateful children ... children like that irritating Nicky who lived two doors down.

Pesky, little whelp, anyway. Always snoopin' around askin' questions, always talking about how friendly the town's people were right from the day he moved in. Well, why didn't he just go harass some of those friendly people and leave her be?

She passed a vacant lot. A few Christmas trees leaned against a makeshift picket fence. The pungent odor of pine assaulted her nostrils, and she wrinkled her nose against the scent. What a waste of money. She wouldn't buy one even if she could afford it. Christmas was like any other day to her, and she would treat it as such right down to her usual bowl of soup for supper.

The blueprint scarf, now dulled with age, worked itself loose from the knot at the base of her throat. Jerking at the frayed cloth, she pulled the material tight about her head, retied the ends, and stuffed some unruly strands of hair behind her ears.

Inadvertently, she thought of the first time she'd seen the bright scarf. Howard had saved up to get it for her for their first Christmas together. She remembered how she'd berated him for spending what little money they had, though it secretly pleased her with his surprise. He had only shrugged and cupped her chin in his big loving hand.

"Say all you want, my little Agnes," he'd said. "But I like how the color makes your blue eyes fairly dance."

The old woman snorted. She wondered what Howard would say about her eyes now, muted and colorless. Many things have changed about his little Agnes since his death. She gave an angry shake of her head. No use dwelling on the past. What good would it do? The past wouldn't help a body live in the present.

Turning the corner, she hastened her steps, blaming her hurried gait on the sudden gust of wind pelting her full in the face. The weather was partly the reason. She would not allow herself to think that another reason might be because of the anonymous giver.

For eleven nights something had materialized on her doorstep with only a light knock to announce its appearance. On the first night, she had yanked open the door, annoyed at having her meager supper interrupted. There on the step lay a brightly wrapped package. Startled, she had looked about to see if she could see anybody. She'd been the cruel brunt of childish pranks before, and she had thought surely this another one.

187

She'd scooted the present across the cement with the toe of her shoe; and, when nothing startling happened, she picked up the box and closed the door. Placing it on the table, she kept a steady eye on it as she ate. Maybe the package was a trick. Maybe someone had gotten the wrong address.

It was bedtime before she'd summoned the courage to open the gift. Inside the box nestled banana bread, lovely smelling chocolate chip banana bread. The kind she used to make. How long had it been since she'd eaten a piece?

She pressed her lips together. She would not allow herself to be taken in, not by Nicky not by anyone. Grabbing a knife, she proceeded to cut the cake into tiny pieces, flushing them down the drain. She hadn't found any needles or razor blades, but that didn't mean there wasn't anything harmful in the ingredients.

The second night she'd found two large cookies on her stoop. One was decorated as jolly Santa Claus, the other a snowman. Again, she looked around for the pranksters. Again, she cut the pastries into little pieces watching them disappear in a swirl of water.

An old woman can't be too careful these days.

The third night revealed three artistically decorated Christmas satin bulbs. Someone had taken the time to adorn the red ornaments with pieces of old jewelry, velvet ribbons, and long tassels. She sat at her table, holding each decoration with great care, admiring their beauty in spite of herself. A corner of her mouth lifted somewhat. The action was the closest thing to a smile that she'd had in years.

This was not a prank. Someone thought of her at the busiest time of year.

All of a sudden, she stuffed the ornaments back into the box and threw the package into the corner of her coat closet. She would not succumb to someone's silly idea.

Even so, each night Agnes had tried to catch the unidentified person, to no avail. And, each night the number of things inside the presents had increased. Last night there were eleven oranges wrapped in a small basket tied with a big red ribbon.

Even though she told herself she didn't care, she mentally checked off a short list of likely suspects. She would not admit to herself that she came to look forward to each evening.

Hurrying down the street, she passed that nettlesome Nicky's house. The unmistakable sound of laughter pelted her ears, and she gritted her teeth.

She hated it! She hated the caroling. She hated the glittering lights; but, most of all, she hated the gaiety.

She grimaced, remembering the first time she had met the boy. She's had her mind on the cost of groceries she held in her arms when the brittle sound of wood knocking against the picket had interrupted her thoughts. Frowning, she glanced up and saw a small boy shuffling toward her, his freckled face almost obscured by his crocheted hat and scarf.

189

He spotted her as she turned down her snow-covered walkway, and his wide smile lit up his expressive, brown eyes. "Hi! My name's Nicholas, but everybody calls me Nicky."

Her indifferent grunt failed to dampen his enthusiastic spirit.

"We moved in that yellow house."

She ignored his outstretched hand pointing to his new home. Undaunted, the boy followed her up to her doorstep. The crunch of new snow under his shiny boots added to her irritation. Grumbling, she fumbled with her house key, dropping it in the snow. Before she had a chance to retrieve it, Nicky scooped the key up and unlocked the door. He followed her inside, looking about the unadorned room.

"Don't you have a Christmas tree or decorations?"

"Nope."

"Why?'

"Don't need any," her anger piqued, she dropped the groceries on the countertop. "Besides, Christmas is a waste of time."

"But, what about your kids? Don't they need Christmas?"

"I don't have kids, or family. If that's any of your business."

"Not anybody? Anybody at all?"

"No."

He stared at her with large dark-brown eyes that suddenly appeared wise for a boy as young as he was. "I'm sorry."

"Well, don't be," she snapped. "I don't need nobody, and nobody needs me."

"Everybody needs somebody," he'd said in a quiet voice.

Since that day his words, "everybody needs somebody," had echoed back to her more times than she cared to admit. Now, almost three weeks later, she still insisted to herself that she needed no one. After Howard, she swore she wouldn't be so vulnerable again. Everybody she'd loved throughout her life left for one reason or another, and she did her best to make sure she'd never be hurt again.

Turning onto her walk, she saw a glow through the windows of her house, and she slowed her steps. There were lights on in her home ... dim lights. She was sure she'd turned everything off before leaving for work. Maybe, someone had broken in. Her heart skipped a beat then sped up. Maybe, they were still there!

She shuffled in the snow with her foot uncovering a broken plank that used to be part of her picket fence. Crouching, she grabbed hold of the board in her bare hands, shaking off as much snow as she could, and held it as a weapon. She eased open her front door, stepping inside just far enough to flip on the lights. What she saw made her hand freeze on the switch. She gasped as she stared into her small living room and kitchen. No one had robbed her. It was the opposite.

A nice turkey tied with a green ribbon sat on her countertop. Mr. and Mrs. Santa Claus, sewn out of cloth, commanded attention in the middle of the kitchen table surrounded with more gifts: oranges and apples, white and sweet potatoes, canned green beans, homemade bread, butter, strawberry jam, chocolates, and a pumpkin pie.

But, it was the sight of the small tree with tiny blinking lights that astounded her.

Dropping the piece of wood, she drew nearer. Without counting, she knew there were twelve ornaments made with the same care as the ones she had angrily tossed down on the floor of her closet.

She hurried to retrieve the box, reverently taking each bulb out, placing it on the tree as soothing strains of Silent Night filtered in from the street.

Agnes didn't know when her turning point occurred. Was it the night she'd found the first present on her step? Or was it the moment she caught sight of the beautiful tree? Maybe, it was the day she'd met Nicky. No matter.

A stirring in her heart spread into a delicious warmth. Somehow, she knew that Nicky and his family were responsible for all this, and she vowed she would find a way to thank them. Joining in with the carolers, she hummed while taking great pleasure watching her tree. She seemed to glow in the soft lights, and if Howard were there, he would say that her blue eyes fairly danced.

Outside in the starry night, Nicky stood nestled between his father and mother. For the past four years they had given the gift of the Twelve Days of Christmas to someone in need, but not to the extent they'd given to Agnes. They had to leave Nicky's grandma behind when they'd moved. His grandma had other grandchildren to share Christmas with, but Agnes had no one. So, Nicky decided to adopt her. Agnes didn't know that yet, but she would ... in time.

When they finished singing their last song, Nicky grinned up at his parents. His dad twinkled his freckled nose before lifting him up onto his shoulders. Then his mom and dad held hands as they took their time walking home. He loved the sound of the snow crunching under his dad's big feet. He loved the tender look on his mother's face when she smiled up at him.

But, most of all, he loved the warm feeling in his heart because they brought Christmas joy to a lonely old lady.

ABOUT the AUTHOR: SHERRY ROSEBERRY

Sherry Roseberry was born and raised in a small town in Idaho. There were two things she wanted to be when she grew up, a mother and an actress. From middle school to college her focus was drama. While in a seventh-grade class, her English teacher said that if they ever wanted to write for magazines like The Readers Digest the articles had to be perfect in spelling, grammar, and punctuation. She admonished the students to take English classes seriously

Roseberry remembers thinking that advice didn't pertain to her because she wasn't going to be a writer. She was going to be an actress! From middle school to college, her focus was drama. Little did she know she would end up writing.

Her drama training hasn't been wasted, though. She's been in several community productions and written, acted in, and sold four plays to Eldridge Play Company. Three are still in print. She has adapted the acting methods she's learned and has given numerous workshops teaching others the same techniques.

Besides her four plays, Roseberry has published articles, short stories, two historical romantic suspense books, and one contemporary romantic suspense book. Now she's concentrating on writing a mystery series with two elderly sister sleuths.

But, she still remembers her seventh grade English teacher. She sure wishes she'd paid more attention.

Her books can be found at sherryroseberry.com

Popcorn Balls
A favorite of Sherry Roseberry

- 2 cups sugar
- 2/3 cup white corn syrup

- 1/2 cup butter (one stick)
- 1 1/2 tsp salt

Cook to hardball stage add:

- 1 1/2 tsp vanilla or peppermint
- 1 tsp cake food coloring of choice

Pour over 2 qts. of popcorn, stir, and form into balls

Million Dollar Fudge
A favorite of Sherry Roseberry

- 4 cups sugar
- 1 large can evaporated milk

Cook until mixture comes to a hard boil. Time and boil for 4 minutes. Remove from heat and add:

- 2 large Hershey chocolate bars
- 2 pkg. chocolate chips
- 1 jar marshmallow creme
- 1 tsp Vanilla
- 1 cup chopped walnuts

Stir until melted and pour into a buttered pan. Makes about 5 lbs.

Microwave Peanut Brittle
A favorite of Sherry Roseberry

- 1 1/2 cup raw peanuts
- 1 cup sugar
- 1/2 cup white corn syrup

At 5 minutes take out and stir well, cook the remaining 2 minutes and stir. Add:

- 1 tbsp butter
- mix, cook 2 more minutes, add:
- 1 tsp vanilla
- 1 tsp baking soda

Spread on buttered cookie sheet, cool, then break into pieces

Fir Trees for Sale

by Carol Curtis Stilz

"We are a family, we three, going to get our Christmas tree," sang my five-year-old daughter, Kathy. She walked between her dad and me as we headed for our car in search for the perfect tree for our new home. This year, we could fit an eight-foot-tree in our living room, unlike last year.

"Do you have rope to tie the tree on top of the Chevy, just in case it doesn't fit in the trunk?" I asked.

"Got it!" Kip said. "This year we'll get a great tree. Rich has a wonderful selection, and proceeds help the scouts in our area."

We pulled into Rich's driveway beside his home. Trees stood tall and straight in rows where well-manicured lawn usually greeted guests.

"Dad, remember we want a *fir* tree," Kathy said with her usual matter-of-fact determination.

"Sure. Rich said he has lots of noble firs this year."

"Ok." She unlatched her car seat, opened the door, and raced for the trees.

I ran to keep up with my sprinting daughter, while Kip shook hands with Rich.

"Mom, I don't see a fir tree."

"We will keep looking. The sign ahead says Noble Firs."

Kip and Rich joined us. "I found you folks three trees that should just fit your new home." Rich led the way down one row and over two more. Three elegant trees towered over us, lush and full, unlike their slender kin the noble firs.

"Oh, Rich, any one would be perfect!" I said.

"Which one do you want to take home, Kathy?" her Dad asked putting his arm around her shoulder.

"None of these trees are fir trees. You promised we could have a fir tree!"

I expected her to stamp her foot or put her hands on her hips. This time her voice said it all without shouting or whining.

Rich stooped down to Kathy's eye level. "I promise these are fir trees. I raised them and cut them myself. I would not want to fool you."

Kathy huffed. "But these trees aren't like Grandma May's fir tree. That's what I want."

"Grandma May's tree?" I asked.

"Yes. I loved her tree. When I touched it the branches felt furry, like my kitty Jake. And it was pink too."

Kip and I looked at each other and stifled our laughter.

"Why are you smiling? Is this a joke?" Kathy demanded.

"No, honey. We just didn't understand what kind of tree you wanted."

Kip said, "Choose a tree you like. I'll make it a furry tree, but maybe white instead of pink. OK?"

"Pink is so pretty. Grandma says it's her favorite color. But I guess white is good too. It'll look like in snowed on the tree." She giggled. "Snow inside our house. That's funny."

Rich added, "Your dad can get the stuff to make your tree fuzzy at a store in town. Do you have a spray gun, Kip?"

"'Fraid not."

"I have one I can loan you." Then Rich turned to Kathy. "Next time I have a little girl request a fir tree, I'll be sure to find out just how furry she wants her tree."

Kathy smiled, and then pointed to the tree nearest her. "This one will make a good fur tree."

That afternoon Kip spent in the garage spraying our tree several times until Kathy approved. The next evening, certain the tree was dry, we brought it in the living room. Jake, our golden Persian cat, looked up and sniffed. I imagined him saying, "Looks kinda like a tree. Smells kinda like a tree. Wonder if I can climb that thing?"

As if reading my thoughts, Kip said, "Before we trim this tree, I need to do one more thing." He hurried to the garage and brought back his drill and sturdy hooks and wire. Once more he disappeared into the garage and brought back a ladder. "Hold the tree, Carol. We'll need to guy wire it on three sides or we'll have a tree and a cat on the floor."

"Kathy, take Jake to your room for a bit. I'll call you when the tree is ready to decorate," I said.

Later that evening Kathy, Kip, and I stood beside our elegant fur tree drenched in lights glimmering like diamonds and ornaments shimmering like silk. Jake curled up beneath on the red velvet tree skirt and snuggled in for a nap. Yes, we had the perfect tree for our family…a fur tree.

Now, our daughter has children of her own, but I still smile every time I see a sign that says Fir Trees for Sale.

ABOUT the AUTHOR: CAROL CURTIS STILZ

Carol enjoys Christmas, writing, gardening, cooking, fishing, solving mysteries, and playing with her grandkids. She loves to create stories with a Christmas theme. For five years she reviewed food products for a newspaper. Carol has shared her interests with others by teaching writing in high school and college in Washington, Montana, and Idaho. She has read her books for children in elementary schools.

GRANDMA BUFFALO, MAY AND ME is available in paperback and as an e-book. Visit carolstilz.com to learn more and contact Carol.

Joy's First Christmas

by Carol Curtis Stilz

Joy spread her new wings and soared into the sky. She fluttered back to close Heaven's gate. This was her first trip to Earth. She felt a little nervous, but she wasn't afraid. The Archangel Gabriel had visited Earth many times. He led the way for all the angels.

Joy moved through space and time at a speed she had not imagined. As she raced past stars, moons, and planets, she kept her eyes on Gabriel. His light was brighter than all the stars.

Darkness spread around her as she neared Earth. Then she saw one incredible brilliant star shining. Beneath her, one tiny point of flame danced on the hillside.

She heard a soft bleating from the sheep that nestled together in a field. Those who tended the sheep warmed themselves by the fire. They looked up and saw Gabriel and the other angels. The shepherds covered their eyes then knelt on the grass.

Joy hovered with the other angels.

"Do not be afraid," Gabriel said. "I bring good news to you and all people, news which will fill you with great joy. The King of Heaven and Earth has been born. He is Christ the Lord, the Son of God. You will find him lying in a manger."

As soon as he had spoken, the angels sang, "Glory to God in the highest and peace to all people."

Joy had never heard the angels sing more sweetly. Her own small voice joined in harmony as they continued singing. She closed her eyes. A note caught in her throat. How she wanted to see this special Baby, God's Son.

Joy had not seen God's face. The other angels had. She wanted with all her heart to see God! The one time she had appeared before Him, she had thought of how little she was and how great He was. The light about Him was brighter than a thousand suns so she had bowed her head. Then she saw the rainbow around God's throne, and it dazzled her. She had gazed at the jewel-like colors instead of God's face.

Then Joy looked around her. Gabriel and the angels were gone. Only seven shepherds remained. One spoke, "Let us go into Bethlehem this night to see the Holy Child."

I'll go with the shepherds to see the Son of God. She followed the sheep.

A small shepherd boy asked, "Who are you?"

"Joy. What's your name?"

"Samuel."

"You see me?"

"Sure, can you see me?"

"Of course, angels see everyone. But I don't believe the others see me."

"Probably not. Some grown-ups miss a lot. If you are an angel, I have a favor to ask you."

"Yes?" She was pleased. No one had asked her for help before.

"Could you teach me that song? I'd like to play it on my flute. It's lonely in these hills. If I knew your song, it would be comforting."

"Of course."

She and Samuel were going to see the Son of God! She sang again and Samuel quickly learned the song on his flute. The shepherds hummed along as they walked to the stable.

They waited at the door. A tall man welcomed them inside. Samuel and Joy tiptoed over the soft earthen floor. A young woman rested against a mound of straw. Next to her, in a manger, lay a tiny bundle.

I wish He would turn His face towards me. Joy fluttered above the shepherds trying to see Him.

The shepherds knelt. Even though Gabriel and the angels had gone, some of Heaven's light remained. Samuel and Joy knelt too.

Mary invited them to move closer. One by one, the shepherds looked at the Baby. Then Samuel and Joy stood beside the manger.

"He's nearly as small as a newborn lamb! What's His name?" Samuel said.

"We call him Jesus," Joseph answered.

"Oh Baby Jesus," Joy whispered. "I wish You would open Your eyes." But Jesus continued to sleep.

A lamb and its mother peeked inside the manger. A shepherd led them outside with the others.

Joseph and Mary gave them a blessing for safe travel and the shepherds left.

"Thank you for coming, Joy and Samuel," Mary whispered.

"We couldn't miss seeing your Son. Thank you." Joy said and they walked outside.

Samuel said, "I'll never forget this night or your song, Joy."

"God gives us songs. He is so pleased when we share them with others. Whenever you play the song, think of Him. I'll see you again, Samuel."

Joy knew she should return to Heaven. The other angels had. But how? She had never been this far from home. Gloria warned her not to wander off, but she had.

Joy tried to remember basic flight instructions. She spread her wings and flew, but only a short distance, not past stars and moons and planets. She landed outside the stable once again. She rubbed her halo, but that only increased the light about her. She put her wings together and pressed her hands together. Nothing happened!

"Isn't there one other angel left on Earth this night?" She searched the night sky for the stars, moons, and planets. Darkness and silence wrapped around her. Her only answer was the cry of a sheep from the hillside beyond Bethlehem. Joy felt tears flowing from her eyes. She was afraid.

She remembered the Baby inside the stable. He had come from Heaven too. He would know the way back, if only He could speak. She glided inside. Mary and Joseph rested against bundles of straw. Joseph's eyes opened and he saw Joy at the manger.

Joy said, "I'll watch Baby Jesus. You and Mary sleep."

Joseph closed his eyes.

Joy stared at the sleeping Infant. She traced the features of His face in her memory. Surely, the Son of God must look like His Father. Joy felt calm. Even though I am a little angel, it will be all right. She watched over the Son of God during His first night on Earth. Softly, she hummed her song. He sighed and she smiled.

Hours passed. The doves cooed in the rafters. "I must be going soon," Joy said to the sleeping Child. "Morning is coming, the first Christmas morning on Earth." She stroked the Baby's face with her finger.

His eyes opened.

Joy hid her face in her trembling hands. "Now I've done it. I've awakened You. Please don't cry, Baby Jesus."

Joy gazed at the Child. Light, like the rainbow about the throne of God, dazzled her. "You know me!" She knew she was loved for who she was a little angel. That was more than enough. Peace flowed through her.

Mary rose and walked forward. "Would you like to hold him?"

"Yes, please!" Joy sat down on the bundle of straw. Mary placed the Baby in her arms. She stared at him. "He's more beautiful than all the stars, moons, and planets combined."

At that moment, Baby Jesus looked into her eyes. His tiny fingers grasped Joy's smallest finger. She closed her eyes. "Thank you, Heavenly Father, for this moment." She looked at the Child and saw the face of God.

She heard the words, "My child, whenever you are frightened or lost, come to Me. I am always with you, but you may not see Me, hear Me, or feel My touch except through others. Be calm. Know I am with you. All is well."

Joy returned Baby Jesus to His mother's arms. "I must go," she said.

Mary nodded and smiled, "Go with God."

Joy bowed her head and prayed, "Heavenly Father, please help me find my way home."

In an instant, she soared past stars, moons, and planets. The light of Heaven guided her home, and on Earth light shone through the darkness.

ABOUT the AUTHOR: CAROL CURTIS STILZ

Carol enjoys Christmas, writing, gardening, cooking, fishing, solving mysteries, and playing with her grandkids. She loves to create stories with a Christmas theme. For five years, she reviewed food products for a newspaper.

Carol has shared her interests with others by teaching writing in high school and college in Washington, Montana, and Idaho. She has read her books for children in elementary schools.

GRANDMA BUFFALO, MAY AND ME is available in paperback and as an e-book. Visit carolstilz.com to learn more and contact Carol.

210

Estralita's Gift

by Carol Curtis Stilz

Estralita patted the precious bundle Grandmother had given her. Grandmother could not travel with her to Christmas Eve Mass since she hurt her foot yesterday. So Grandmother said, "Take these gifts to church. Place them on the altar for Baby Jesus on His birthday."

Then Estralita joined her aunt, uncle and cousin, Roberto, for the journey to the mission on this Holy Night. They walked beside their neighbors in the procession that led from their homes on the hillside to the village in the valley.

Estralita looked up at the night sky, wondering if she might see a star as bright as the star of Bethlehem. "Look Roberto! The stars look like flowers in the fields where we play in summer."

"And the little lanterns beside the path look like fallen stars to guide us," he answered.

Looking into the darkness beyond the lanterns, Estralita saw a small figure in the shadows. She heard crying. Estralita stepped toward the child. "Why are you crying?"

"I have not eaten today. Mama says there is no food in our house."

Estralita patted her precious bundle. She remembered how she felt when she was hungry. Grandmother had said they were blessed because they had food when some people did not. Then Estralita untied the knot and brought forth a large corncake. "No one should be hungry at Christmas." She gave the girl most of the cake, saving only a small piece which she wrapped in her bundle.

"Bless you!" said the child and she disappeared in the darkness.

Estralita patted her bundle, now much smaller than before. "It will be enough." Grandmother said, "What is given in love is always enough. Our humble gifts to the Baby Jesus become holy in His sight."

She ran to catch up with Roberto. Before she had gone far, she heard a beggar calling, "Child, can you spare a coin or two? I am an old man and cannot harvest the crops any longer. I am alone, tired and hungry."

Estralita patted her precious bundle. She remembered how she felt when she was tired and hungry. Grandmother had said they were blessed to have each other and a hacienda whose shelves were filled with food. Then Estralita untied the knot and gave the man most of the corncake. Then she untied another knot and withdrew a shiny gold coin.

"No one should be alone and tired and hungry at Christmas." She gave the coin to the old man.

"Bless you!" said the old man and he disappeared in the darkness.

Estralita stopped to tie up the tiny piece of corncake. She remembered her grandmother's words, "What is given in love is always enough."

"I trust it is so," said Estralita to the bright stars.

Then Estralita heard a squeak. She looked down to see a small mouse. Estralita was sure she heard the mouse say, "I have nothing to feed my children. Please, spare a few crumbs."

Estralita touched her precious little bundle. She opened the kerchief that held the bit of corncake. Then she gathered the crumbs in her hand and sprinkled them on the ground beside the mouse.

She was sure the mouse squeaked, "Bless you, child. My children thank you as I do." Then the mouse disappeared in the darkness.

Estralita looked at her empty kerchief. Grandmother had trusted her to take a gift to the Baby Jesus. "What can I give Him now?" she said to the bright stars above. "How I wish you were flowers. You look so close that I could touch the sky and a gather a bouquet for Mary and Baby Jesus."

213

She looked ahead and saw the small bonfires that marked the entrance to the mission tonight. Desperately, Estralita looked on the ground, searching for a fallen coin or small piece of cake, anything she could give to the Baby Jesus. All she saw were bushes of green leaves growing beside the road. These plants were ones Grandmother called wild weeds.

As she stared at the entrance to the mission where a patch of the weeds were especially thick, she looked into the eyes of a statue. Estralita said, 'Why you are an angel. Everyone should see you on this Holy Night. Instead, you are hidden in weeds."

Estralita cleared away the weeds so everyone could see the stone angel. Very softly she said, "How I wish you were a real angel. You could help me. I have no gift for the Baby Jesus. Where can I find one now when I am so close to the mission? Mass will begin soon."

Then she heard a voice that seemed to come from the angel. "Wrap these weeds in your kerchief. Give them to the Christ Child. He will bless them and you for your gift is given in love."

Estralita quickly gathered the weeds. She wrapped her kerchief around the ends of the stems.

Then she ran to catch up with Roberto. When she again walked beside him, he asked her, "What is in your bundle? It looks larger than before."

Estralita hesitated. Then she pulled back the folds of the kerchief. She stared at the drooping leaves. "Oh, no! They are wilting."

"Is this your gift? Dead leaves?" said Roberto. "Well, Grandmother said, 'What is given in love is always enough.' She is old and wise, so I hope it is so."

Estralita wrapped the kerchief around the wilted leaves. She entered the courtyard of the mission. She found water left for animals to drink. She dipped the stems in the water. Then she wrapped up the branches in her kerchief and stepped inside the church.

Estralita prayed silently, "Baby Jesus. You know how much Grandmother loves You. Please see this small gift as if it were flowers as abundant and bright as the stars in the sky this Hold Night."

Estralita knelt at the altar before the Christ Child's crib. She looked at the face of the Baby Jesus smiling back at her. Then she placed her kerchief beside the other gifts. She drew back the folds of fabric and held her breath.

On the altar she saw bright red flowers in the shape of stars. Every flower contained a tiny cluster of gold, as if her small coin had multiplied in the heart of each blossom.

Behind her she heard people murmur, "Look! It's a miracle. Those wilted weeds became beautiful crimson flowers before our eyes."

Estralita heard the priest repeat the words Grandmother had said, "What is given in love is always enough. Our humble gifts to the Christ Child become holy in His sight."

When Estralita and Roberto stepped outside the mission, they saw the stone angel surrounded by bright fiery red flowers.

"See! Roberto said, as he pointed to the path they had followed. The lights from the little lanterns illumined the hundreds of star flowers marking their way.

Two centuries later Estralita's gift, given in love, is a part of Christmas celebrations in many lands. Her gift is called Flowers of the Holy Night or Poinsettias.

Note: Many versions of the legend of the poinsettia exist today. I read a simple five-line account in 2000. Then I remembered an image written by my grandfather, Raphael (Ray) Curtis. Flowers in the field are the stars of heaven fallen to earth. I considered that image and looked outside. Through the window I saw the magnificent angel statue sculpted by my housemate, Maryann Inman. This story seemed to flow through me that afternoon. "Estralita's Gift" became my Christmas greeting that December.

ABOUT the AUTHOR: CAROL CURTIS STILZ

Carol enjoys Christmas, writing, gardening, cooking, fishing, solving mysteries, and playing with her grandkids. She loves to create stories with a Christmas theme. For five years she reviewed food products for a newspaper. Carol has shared her interests with others by teaching writing in high school and college in Washington, Montana, and Idaho. She has read her books for children in elementary schools.

GRANDMA BUFFALO, MAY AND ME is available in paperback and as an e-book. Visit carolstilz.com to learn more and contact Carol.

SANDWICH COOKIES FOR SANTA

This sandwich cookie for Santa's plate is quick and easy. The easiest to assemble of four variations uses store bought round sugar cookies to hold the frosting filling that can also be store bought.

The refrigerated sugar cookie dough provides another shortcut. Just follow the directions on the package. Another quick method for making the "sandwich" uses cookies made from cake mix. The last version uses your own favorite sugar cookie recipe. The filling can be any of your favorite frostings tinted a Christmassy color. My favorite is a cream cheese crushed candy cane filling that follows below.

For the store-bought cookies, spread your favorite frosting to hold the cookies together, and that's it. Bake the refrigerated dough cookies using the size you prefer for your cookies. If making your own from scratch, make and bake as usual.

I've used the cake mix variation to produce 24 to 48 sandwich cookies depending on size. Often, I make two batches for bake sales and they sell out. *I use a variation of a recipe found in TASTE OF HOME 1997 Annual Recipes, credited to Karen Bourne of Magrath, Alberta*

INGREDIENTS

- 2 packages (18-1/4 ounces each) cake mix - I like red velvet at Christmas)
- 4 eggs, lightly beaten
- 2/3 cup vegetable oil
- 1 package (8ounces) cream cheese
- ½ cup butter or margarine, softened
- 3-4 cups confectioners' sugar
- ½ teaspoon vanilla extract
- Red food color, optional

Beat the cake mixes, eggs, and oil in a large mixing bowl. Roll into 1-inch balls. Place on ungreased baking sheets and flatten slightly. Bake for 8-10 minutes or until a slight indentation remains when touched. Cool. The cookies will have a crackle finish rather than smooth surface.

In another mixing bowl, beat cream cheese and butter or margarine. Add sugar and vanilla. Mix until smooth. Tint with food coloring. I use red. If no coloring is added the mixture is white or slightly yellow.

Crush 4-6 candy canes until fine, somewhere between the texture of sugar and Kosher salt. Spread frosting on bottom of half the cookies. Sprinkle crushed candy canes on frosting. I spread a dab on the underside of top cookies for a good bond to bottom of sandwich.

Santa and his helpers will enjoy these "sandwiches".

MERRY CHRISTMAS!

219

MY GUARDIAN

by Kitten O'Ryan

On December 18, 1979, I celebrated my twenty-first birthday. It started off as a day of happy celebration with friends and family. It ended with sorrowful regret.

A blistery wind dropped the winter night's chill-factor well below zero. This was rare in the state of Ohio, but of course it would happen on my birthday. Such was my luck. After an afternoon of shopping, styling hair, and putting on makeup, I stood before the mirror for one last examination.

I looked very enticing in my brand-new outfit. Man-Hunting was definitely on my agenda and, with the image I saw in the mirror, it was going to be a piece of cake. And I'm not talking *birthday* cake either!

Giddy with joy, I was excited to go out. After all, this was going to be my first *legitimate* trip to a bar.

My best friend, Pam, would soon pick me up. Since it was my birthday, she'd insisted on being the designated driver. Okay, maybe I twisted her arm. I just figured my childhood friend owed me one, as I had always been there for her.

She agreed.

And this is *our* story ....

"Come in," I shouted, knowing Pam would enter.

"Are you ready?" she asked as she entered the living room. She stopped in her tracks when she saw me. "Wow, you look nice!"

Her gaze dropped to my feet to study the black and gold spaghetti-strap shoes that attempted to cover them. "Seriously? It's twenty degrees outside; it might even snow later."

"I know. But we're going to be *inside* dancing and drinking; maybe play some darts, or pool, or my all-time favorite, Foosball;

then more dancing." I rotated my hips. "They'll work for all that, won't they?"

Pam rolled her eyes. "Whatever." She tossed her keys on the coffee table and stuck out her hand. "The El Camino's keys please."

I donned my coat and hat. Reaching into my right pocket, I pulled out my out-of-town boyfriend's keys and slapped them into her palm. "Steve said to be careful. He just got it out of the shop last week."

"Should be him driving us around. What kind of boyfriend would rather work than take his new girlfriend out for her birthday?"

"The noncommittal casual kind," I said with a chuckle. I opened the door. Frigid air slapped me across the face. "It's flipping freezing!" I shivered. "Brrr! We're going to have to be careful driving tonight; the roads will probably get icy."

"They're already icy."

It took us about a half-hour to simply drive to downtown Columbus and I was never more relieved when we finally turned into the parking lot of our favorite nightclub, Fibber McKees. Fibber McKees was not only popular with the Ohio State college kids, but the young professionals snared it as a favorite hangout too. Luckily, Pam found a parking spot right by the door. That way if it snowed or sleeted later, my open-toed feet wouldn't get as wet.

Entering through the heavy wooden doors, Bob Seger's raspy voice greeted us, as the song *Old Time Rock and Roll* blared from the jukebox. The friends we were meeting saw us and waved us over to the table they'd been saving. Shrugging out of our coats, we hung them over the chair backs, sat down, and started visiting.

Preordered drink in hand, I scanned the room. The place was crowded.

Conversation streamed from our midsized group of eight, as most of us hadn't been together in over a month. We updated one another on our daily mishaps and adventures, various job victories and fiascos, and who was dating who and why.

Our table was definitely the fun table. We laughed and laughed.

And the drinks kept flowing.

221

As the night went on, the music and crowd-roar intensified. It took strong lungs and great effort to be heard.

Pam stood and spoke loud enough to be understood above the near record-high-decibel mayhem. "I'm going to go dance with Ed."

"Who?" I asked.

"You know him, Kit." She tipped her head toward the actual bar part of the club, "The guy sitting on the stool at the end."

I noticed the handsome, somewhat burly man sporting a huge Cheshire grin beneath a well-trimmed mustache. "Sure...Ed...I get ya now. The good-looking guy I've passed by all night on the way to the bathroom." I took a drink. "Say hi to our *good* friend, Ed, for me."

As Pam joined Ed's side, four of us rather inebriated girls slipped from the booth. It was time to play some serious Foosball. After a couple of games, then we planned to head out onto the newly waxed dancefloor to shake our booties.

I had no problem finding dance partners. Man-Hunting was as easy as I'd predicted at home. I remember thinking I should have bought my new outfit months ago.

The night sped by fast.

Too fast.

Before I knew it, the bartender announced, "Last Call," over the microphone.

Drunk as a skunk, I scanned the crowd for my designated driver. I finally saw her heading toward me, stumbling a bit. I knew Pam had been drinking more than a couple drinks.

"Are you okay to drive?" I asked once she stood before me.

She raised her forearm, airborne hand waving down, in a way to silently say, *really?*

"I'm just fine."

There wasn't a single slur evident in her words.

Perhaps I had simply imagined the stumbling.

"Let's blow out of here," she ordered.

That said, she walked to the table, grabbed her coat off the back of the empty chair, and shrugged inside it.

I copied her actions and, together, we shoved our way out the doors.

222

It *had* snowed while we were inside. Patchy white areas gave proof to that. But now a frozen rain drizzled from the sky. The temperature had dropped at least ten more degrees.

The roads were now going to be *extremely* slippery.

We got to the car and climbed inside. Pam started the engine, revved it a couple times, flicked on the heater to begin defrosting the windshield, and then exited to scrape the windows. Lips blue, skin pale, she looked frozen by the time she got back inside the car.

As we pulled from our parking spot, the Camino's tires couldn't grip the ice-covered asphalt and we slid sideways toward the street. Exiting the parking lot, we had to creep down the city streets so as not to swerve into the opposite lane of traffic or the sidewalks beside us. Truly, it felt as though we could have walked faster than our car was traveling.

Finally, through the busier part of the city, the speed limit increased to 50mph. However, Pam kept the car around 35mph, which seemed like a record-breaking pace compared to the tedious crawl we'd been traveling only minutes earlier. We neared our turnoff: Olentangy River Rd.

Little did either of us know that our lives were about to change.

After cautiously making the turn, Pam slowly gained speed. "The road feels good," she whispered. "I think it'll be fine to go the posted speed. Don't you?"

"They look dry, but I'm not touching the wheel, so I'll have to take your word for it." Feeling a tad queasy, having eaten little and drank much, I cracked open the window to inhale deeply of the frigid air.

We were nearing the familiar, long, guardrail-protected curve in the road that was a breeze to navigate in normal weather.

And that's when it happened.

The shine of the Black Ice became visible seconds before we began sliding. Pam turned the wheel in the opposite direction and gave it gas to compensate.

But it didn't work.

We hit the guardrail at about 50mph, the car slithering against it with the hideous sound of mashing metal against metal. Looking out my window, all I saw were orange sparks. I heard someone scream and realized the scream must have come from me.

I was told in the hospital that we took out three-hundred feet of guardrail before crashing through a light pole and flipping three times down the once-protected ravine. The car came to rest on top of a piece of heavy machinery.

"You okay, Pam?" I managed to ask through a mouth that was swelling as quickly as a balloon being pumped full of helium; a mouth that tasted like blood and felt wet with the same fluid.

She didn't say a single word.

"Pam!" Tears filled my eyes.

Fear filled my heart. "Pam?"

Nothing.

Then I heard it…a gurgling sound that resembled wisps of air only minus the oxygen. Then I realized it came from my left. *Pam? Was she drowning?*

"Pam…you need to wake up and breathe!"

Tears slipped down my cheeks, as silence was my only answer.

I can't remember how long the unnatural sound lasted.

I can't remember when it stopped.

But it did.

And the only audible sound became the icy wind whipping through the broken windows.

It was then I realized we were upside down in the car.

"Help me," I tried to shout, but the words that passed between my lips were more of a hoarse garble.

It was then I saw a white-robbed figure that seemed to glow in the darkness. Face obscured, I felt as though someone caressed the crown of my head. I felt loved, protected, and unbelievably safe. My world darkened in the midst of this strange unexplainable happening.

I don't know how long Pam and I hung from our seatbelts before help arrived. The next thing I knew, I felt a tug on my coat as though someone was trying to pull me out of the car.

Lots of voices went in and out of my conscious-seeking thoughts; sirens filled the air.

Someone took hold of my wrist. "I got a pulse!"

"No pulse here," another voice announced opposite my seat.

Someone's comforting voice registered through the confusion.

"Close your eyes, lady, and we'll get you out of here."

The sound of a motor. Tearing metal. The smell of fuel. Smoky oily gas.

I struggled to comprehend what was happening.

The sound of the door giving way brought me from my mind's swirling fog.

"You're okay. Hold on, darlin'. The *Jaws of Life* opened up a way for us to extricate, but I still have to cut you out of the seatbelt."

I heard fabric rip seconds before the strap gave. Strong arms encircled my waist before pulling me free of the wreckage.

I saw my human angel's face: a man with compassionate eyes…a man who seemed not much older than me. "Don't let me die," I told him.

"Not on my watch," he answered, as he laid me on a board and strapped me to it.

"Don't leave me." I gripped the cuff his long-sleeved shirt.

Warmth covered the back of my hand. "I'll be beside you the whole way to the hospital. I promise." I was then lifted into what I thought was a van, but in reality was an ambulance.

I hadn't fully realized Pam was dead, but I had a horrific feeling that she was. I tried not to think about the possibility, choosing to stare into the eyes of my heroic rescuer instead.

Later, at the hospital, I finally asked the doctor. "Where's Pam?"

"She didn't make it."

Shock kept me silent until I was in my room and my dad showed up.

I ended up with a fractured back, bruising in my ribcage and torn ligaments in my right knee with embedded glass in my face and torso. Though I was in serious pain, compared to Pam, I was in great shape—I was alive.

Later, the detectives arrived to ask me about the accident. It was then I learned Pam's alcohol level had been high - two and a half times the legal limit. Coupled with the bad weather, that created a toxic driving combination resulting in the accident and Pam's untimely death.

They asked a slew of questions. I answered them the best I could, but they kept asking me the strangest question of all…*Was anyone else with you girls?*

My answer of *no* must have not registered with them, because they asked it several times. I repeatedly answered the same way until I became frustrated, shouting a final, "NO!"

My daddy sensed my frustration and asked them why they weren't accepting my answer, to which they replied, "Several people told us they saw someone all dressed in white cross the road near the ravine. We just want to make sure we didn't leave anyone else out there."

It was then I remembered my white robed visitor...the visitor that brought me peace in the most chaotic time of my life. I thought to myself it must have been an angel.

December 18, 1979 is a time I will never forget. It gave me PTSD: fear of driving, fear of dying; fear of ever hearing that awful gurgling sound again. There was a sense of creepiness that I'd been beside a lifeless body for who knows how long. Then there was the guilt for feeling that creepiness and guilt for not realizing Pam should not have been driving that night. Finally, there was sorrow...such an unbelievable sadness that I had lost my best friend forever.

My relationship with Steve ended with the destruction of his car. I never saw him again after the wreck.

Though years have passed, I still struggle with the issues I took with me from that fateful night. But it was also the night my Guardian Angel showed up to save my life and took my precious Pam to her eternal home—Heaven.

Thanks for reading!
We hope you have enjoyed our
Christmas collection.
Merry Christmas to all!

Made in United States
North Haven, CT
20 August 2024

56340535R00140